SOME

M

Warwic

This is a work of fiction. Similarities to real people, places, or events are entirely coincidental.

SOME THEY LIE

First edition. July 2, 2018.

Copyright © 2018 M.K. Farrar.

ISBN: 978-1725534292

Written by M.K. Farrar.

To Rachel McClellan, whose generosity meant I never let this book go.

Chapter One
Present Day

THE MAN HUNG BY HIS wrists from an iron hook embedded in the ceiling.

She stood in front of him, staring, contemplating her next move. His jaw pressed against his bare chest, creating the appearance of a double chin where normally there was none. Unconscious, for the moment, his whole body hung loose and slack. Because of the low ceiling, the toes of his boots skated against the floor, giving him the barest modicum of relief from the pressure in his wrists and shoulders, but only when he was conscious enough to balance.

The rope securing his wrists didn't keep her safe. It was the gag between his lips that kept danger at bay, though she knew if he ever managed to work it free, things would be different. He'd affected her already, made her do things she'd never believed herself capable of, and she wouldn't make that same mistake twice.

Red stripes licked across his naked torso, the result of the cane she'd been forced to use. She needed answers, and while she couldn't risk removing the gag, there were other ways she could get him to reply. His refusal to give her anything had made her hurt him, but still he shook his head in defiance every time she asked him what she needed to know. She took no pleasure in the job, but she had to be brave. It was all she had left, and she wouldn't let this man—this *monster*—win.

She was stronger than that.

He'd underestimated the lengths she'd go to in order to make things right. Even with everything on his side, all of his power, she'd still managed to overcome him.

The man let out a muffled groan and began to stir.

Nerves jangled through her system, and the sour taste of fear coated her tongue. As he woke, her pulse quickened, her breath growing shallow in her lungs. She tightened her fingers around the cane and rolled out her neck and shoulders. It was physical work her body wasn't used to, and tension knotted her muscles. As she lifted her arms, her shirt sleeve rode down, exposing the flash of white bandages and the striking slash of red where the blood had seeped through. This was taking its toll on her, but she had to continue until she got what she wanted.

It was time to start again.

Chapter Two
Five Weeks Earlier

"FROM NOW ON, LIV, I'M going to tell you a time half an hour earlier than when we need to leave, just so I know you're going to be ready on time."

Olivia Midhurst looked to where her friend, Ellen, was standing in the doorway, one hand on her hip, her lips pressed together with disapproval.

"I know. I'm sorry." Liv hopped around her bedroom, trying to shove her foot into her black high heel. "I never mean to be so late. I'm just a really bad judge of how long it takes to do things."

Ellen's eyebrows lifted. "How old are you now?"

"Twenty-seven years is nowhere near enough time to learn things," she protested. "And anyway, you were late for coffee the other day."

"Ryan's car broke down, and he couldn't give me a lift. I think that was a reasonable excuse."

"Okay, okay. I'm ready now, though, see?" Olivia straightened and put her hands out either side of her, displaying the little black dress she wore. "Ta-da."

"You look gorgeous, as always." Ellen jerked her head towards the front door, causing her blonde bob to swish against her jawline. "Now, are we going, or what? The poor taxi driver has either given up and left or fallen asleep at the wheel."

Olivia snatched up her clutch bag. "Yes, we're going."

They were meeting some friends, who were also work colleagues, in central London. Olivia normally tried to stay away from the centre of the city—there were too many tourists around—but a DJ one of them loved was playing at one of the central clubs, so she'd been roped along. Her outfit probably wasn't suitable for jumping around a hot, crowded room, but the dance scene wasn't really her thing. She was hoping to drag one or more of her friends off to a Soho wine bar before the night was over.

"Where's Tammy?" Ellen asked as they left the flat to head down to the waiting cab. Knowing Olivia didn't trust the lift, they automatically took the stairs. "Is she out tonight as well?"

Tammy was Olivia's flatmate. While Tammy was blonde, like Ellen, the similarities ended. Ellen was short and curvy, and loved nothing more than spending the weekends playing house with her boyfriend, Ryan, where Tammy was tall and willowy and spent all weekend partying.

"Yeah, she met some guy in a bar last weekend, and now he's wining and dining her. He's one of those city-types she likes." Liv shrugged. "She's happy, but I'll put anything on him being married."

Ellen smacked her with her purse. "Don't be so negative! He might be great. Not all guys are total shits, you know."

"I know, I know. You found one of the good ones."

"Ryan has his faults, but I can trust him. And you'll find someone, too, one day. I know you will."

Liv gave a mock shudder. "No, thanks. I'm happy on my own. Men are only good for one thing, and it's not their brain." She gave Ellen a lewd wink and nudged her with her elbow, and Ellen gave a squeal.

"You're so bad!"

Being able to pick up almost any guy she set her eyes on was a new thing for Olivia. She'd been an awkward child, with her red curly hair, pale skin, and freckles. Always tall and skinny, she'd developed a way of standing, hunched over, so as not to be noticed. Of course, that hadn't worked. The more she'd tried not to be noticed, the more people had focused on her. By people, she meant the popular girls at school. The boys really *had* ignored her—they'd done that without her even trying. But the girls were a different story. If you didn't tick the boxes—pretty, popular, clever—you might as well have committed social suicide at school.

It wasn't until later, after everything had happened, that she'd reinvented herself. To her surprise, she'd learned adulthood had meant being lanky was a good thing, and the breasts she hadn't fully developed until she'd been way past the age of eighteen might be small, but they were enough to be desired. She'd discovered hair products that transformed her frizz into sought-after curls, and spray tans to give her pale skin some colour. But it was her attitude that really made the difference. Keeping her chin up, smiling, making eye contact, and faking confidence. *That* was what was important.

Imposter syndrome. Liv had it in spades. She wished she could be one of those women who didn't care what people thought of her, but she thrived on the approval of others.

They caught the cab into the centre of the city and hopped out. Already, a small queue of people waited to get into the club, though to Liv it looked as though most of them were a decade younger than she was. She hadn't been like these teenagers when she was eighteen. Her life had been far more serious back then, so she figured she deserved to make up for it now.

The two women waited in line, before paying their entrance fee and stepping inside the club. It was already busy, and too loud for Liv, though she smiled and tried to look as though she belonged.

"There they are," Ellen yelled in her ear, pointing across the throng of people and flashing lights toward a small group at the bar.

They pushed their way through. The club smelled of stale sweat, old alcohol, and desperation. Some people might have been there to have a good time, but most were there in the hope of hooking up with someone by the end of the night. Liv felt eyes on her as she walked through, being assessed as a possible screw by the men, and competition by the women. Instinctively, she sucked in her stomach and lifted her chin, trying not to feel the way she was being mentally undressed. The people they were meeting—another woman, Callie, and two of the guys she worked with in the estate agent's office—spotted them. The men were outnumbered now that she and Ellen had arrived. She didn't think they minded. Though nothing had been said out loud, one of the men, Stevie, was as camp as they came, and the other guy, Philip, had never mentioned having a girlfriend. Perhaps he was still in the closet, but he and Stevie were definitely closer than two platonic males normally were. Not that it was any of her business, of course.

"We'd almost given up on you," Callie yelled as they approached. The music was at the sort of volume where everything spoken for the next few hours would have to be done at shouting level.

"Yeah, sorry, my fault," Liv hollered back. "I was running late."

"It's almost eleven."

She gave a shrug. *What can you do?*

"No Tony tonight, then?" Liv asked, mentioning their boss.

Callie rolled her eyes. "No, thank God. I was a bit worried he was going to invite himself along when he heard us all talking about coming here, but then he turned around and walked back into his office."

Ellen laughed. "Thank fuck for that. No one wants their boss coming along on a night out."

Callie's eyebrows shot up her forehead. "Especially not a boss like Tony."

"Aw, come on," Liv said, sticking up for the man who'd given her a chance. "He's not that bad."

"Are you kidding me?" Callie pulled a face. "The man is in his forties, and I'm not sure he has a single friend to speak of, and he's probably never had a girlfriend. Honestly, I don't know how he ended up in the selling business, and especially not as the boss."

"That's the thing," Ellen said. "He has us to run around selling the houses, while he coordinates everything in the background." She shrugged. "He doesn't need a personality for that, just good organisational skills."

Callie flipped her long chestnut hair over her shoulder. The other woman was older than they were by a few years, in her thirties rather than twenties, but hadn't yet settled down. "Well, either way, I'm glad he's not here. It's one thing seeing him at work, but having him around socially gives me the creeps."

Olivia smacked her on the arm. "Don't be so mean. He's not that bad."

Callie drew back her lips in a grimace. "You date him, then."

Liv laughed. They both knew there was no way any of them would be dating Tony Payne.

Someone bought a line of shots, and Liv found herself licking salt, biting down on lime, and grimacing. She could handle a couple of drinks, but no more than that. She was careful to pace herself, knowing too much didn't agree with her. The alcohol quickly did its job, giving her the confidence she normally had to fake, and she found herself being tugged through the throng of clubbers and out onto the dance floor.

Liv danced, surrounded by her colleagues, hands in the air, bodies bumping. She'd even managed to forget how unsuitable her footwear was, though in her heels she was taller than everyone else—even most of the men. The club was hot with all the grinding bodies, and her hair grew damp and clung to the back of her neck and forehead. With surprise, she realised she was actually having a good time.

Her skin prickled with the sensation of someone watching her, and she scanned the crowd. Being recognised by someone was something she dreaded. She'd come to London because it was a big enough city to get lost in. Only a small percentage of people she came across in the city were actually from here. Instead, she was surrounded by a ragtag crew of people from all over the world. It was accepted that you would never get to meet their families, or friends they went to school with. You got their general story, and that was enough. No one ever bothered to look any deeper.

She caught someone watching her, and her heart jackknifed, but for all the right reasons. He stood alone, taking a swig of his bottle of expensive imported beer, all the while never taking his eyes off her. Unlike most of the people here who were casually dressed, this guy still wore what looked like a made-to-measure suit. It was a Friday night, so she guessed he must have been dragged out for drinks directly after finishing work.

Liv glanced away, pretending not to have noticed him, and continued to dance with her work colleagues. She glanced back to the spot where the man had been, and her stomach dipped with disappointment. The man had gone.

Oh, well.

He'd looked cute, but he was just another guy. There were plenty of them around.

She turned around, planning to get another drink, and found him directly behind her.

"Oh!"

He smiled, revealing teeth that could only have been professionally whitened. "I'm sorry. I didn't mean to make you jump. I wondered if I could buy you a drink?"

Liv looked round to find Ellen grinning and waggling her eyebrows at her.

"Um, yeah, sure. Thanks."

She followed him to the bar, admiring the way he moved through the crowd, as though his presence alone made people step out of the way. His shoulders looked great in the suit jacket, though she thought he must have been hot, and she sneaked a look down to see if his arse matched the rest of him. The bottom of the jacket hid most of it, but she figured it was good to leave some things up to the imagination.

They lined up, side by side, at the bar.

"What can I get you?" He had to shout to be heard above the music. She caught a whiff of his cologne—something spicy and expensive, like the rest of him.

"Just half a lager, thanks." She'd only had the one shot of tequila so far, so a small beer wasn't going to hurt. She made a mental note of it, however, not wanting to lose track.

"Peroni?" he said, naming one of the brands.

She nodded. "Thanks."

He signalled the bartender and ordered the drinks.

"What's your name?" He had to lean in close to make himself heard, so she felt the heat of his breath brush against her ear.

"Olivia," she told him. "Most people call me Liv."

"Liv," he repeated with a smile. "I like that. I'm Michael."

"Do people call you Mike for short?" She flirted with a flip of her hair over one shoulder.

He shook his head. "No, it's Michael."

"Oh, right." She wasn't sure what to say to that. Thankfully, her drink was pushed toward her on the bar, and she was able to distract herself by picking up the beer and taking a sip. It was cold, fizzy, and refreshing. Just what she needed after all the dancing.

She glanced across the club to see her friends still on the dance floor. Ellen was keeping an eye on her, making sure the guy in the suit wasn't a complete weirdo. Her friend gave her a little wave, and Liv held back a grin.

The man—Michael, not Mike—turned from the bar so they were both facing the same way. He leaned in to shout in her ear. "Do you go clubbing much?"

"Not really. You don't look like this is your usual haunt either." She motioned at the suit.

He laughed. "No, it isn't. I got dragged out by one of the younger guys at work. He got a promotion and wanted to celebrate."

"Where is he now?"

Michael shrugged. "No idea. Last I heard, he was puking in the toilet. I figured I'd leave him to it."

Liv wrinkled her nose. "I don't blame you."

"Can I buy you a drink somewhere a little more civilised? There's a wine bar around the corner that will still be open."

She smiled. "Yeah, that would be great. Let me go and tell my friend where I'm going. We're sharing a taxi back to Shepherd's Bush, and she'll be mad if I disappear on her."

It was her way of letting him know she wouldn't be going home with him tonight, but also making sure he knew someone would miss her if she didn't show back up. A single woman in the city, she needed to take precautions.

"I'll make sure I get you back safely."

Liv ran up to Ellen and dragged her off to one side to tell her what was happening.

"Okay, but be careful," Ellen yelled back. "He looks hot, but it's often the ones you don't expect who are the psychos."

Liv laughed, thinking how true that statement was. "I've got my phone. I'll call you as soon as we're done, okay?"

"Sure. Have fun, honey!"

She hugged her friend, and tried not to think about the sweaty imprint Ellen's cheek had left on hers.

She found Michael waiting for her near the exit. He put out his elbow for her, an old-fashioned gesture, and she smiled and took it. Relieved to be out of the noisy, hot, sweat-permeated club, she inhaled a lungful of fresh air. They walked a few streets until they found a wine bar which catered to only a handful of customers at this time of night.

"Do you drink red wine?" he asked as they were seated at a table. "Or are you a white drinker?"

"Honestly, I'm happy with either."

"I'll get red, then, shall I?" He lifted a hand to signal the waitress, and she re-appeared with a wide smile. "Can we have a bottle of your New Zealand Pinot Noir?"

Liv flapped a hand. "Oh, just a glass is fine for me." Mentally, she calculated what she'd already had. The shot of tequila, the half a lager, and one glass of red wine. That was enough for her. Perhaps most single women her age would be drinking their own body weight in alcohol on a night out, but Liv was meticulous about the number of units she drank.

But he waved away her concerns. "I'm sure I can manage more than a glass. We can always leave anything we don't drink."

A blush heated her cheeks. "Yeah, okay. That's fine."

The waitress returned with the bottle, and Liv was relieved when she poured a drop into Michael's glass to taste. She had no idea about wines, really, and would have been mortified to accept a bottle, only for the handsome man sitting opposite to say it was off.

He nodded to accept the wine, and the waitress filled their glasses. Michael picked up his and lifted it towards Liv in a salute. "To making new friends."

She copied his actions and clinked hers against his. "Making new friends," she parroted.

He sat back in his seat, his head tilted slightly to one side as he regarded her. "So, tell me everything there is to know about you, Liv."

She laughed, a little embarrassed at the scrutiny. "There isn't really much to tell." Or at least there wasn't much she was *able* to tell him. "I'm twenty-seven, and I'm an estate agent."

"Have you been doing that long?"

She shrugged. "A few years now. I enjoy it. Means I'm not stuck inside an office all day every day. What about you?"

"Recruitment." He leaned in, conspiratorial. "And will you think differently of me if I tell you I'm thirty-four?"

She pulled a face but was teasing. Flirting. "Thirty-four, huh? Practically an old man."

He mock shuddered. "Pension will be on the horizon soon."

They both laughed.

They sipped the wine as they talked. Liv was relieved the conversation flowed with places they'd travelled to—his were far more exotic than hers, though she managed to come up with some stories a few of the younger crowd at work had recounted to her—what foods they liked, television shows, and books.

Her phone buzzed, and she realised the last hour had flown by.

"Sorry," she told him as she checked her mobile. People checking their phones while they talked was a pet hate of hers. It was a message from Ellen. "My friend is expecting me."

He shrugged. "No problem."

She looked at the message, expecting Ellen to be complaining about her not having called yet, but it was something different.

Heading on somewhere else, honey. Call me if you want to join us. Have fun with Mr Tall Dark and Handsome. Be safe.

Liv hid a smile.

"Everything okay?" Michael enquired.

"Yes, fine." She was tempted to stay, to order another bottle of wine, and sit, feeling glamorous and desired opposite this gorgeous, intense man who seemed to hang on her every word. But she knew how it would end—with her getting too drunk and losing control, and then everything would go wrong. It had happened before, and she didn't want it happening again. Especially not with this guy. Some of the men she'd picked up in the past were nothing to her—antipodeans who were travelling and passed their time by working in bars and partying. They were fine for one night, and most of the time she wouldn't have even been able to remember their names. But this guy was different. He was sophisticated, classy. She wanted him to think she was, too.

"I have to get going," she said, regretting her words with every syllable, but knowing it was the right thing to do. "I've got things to do in the morning."

"Oh, of course. I totally understand." Did she see a flicker of regret across his handsome features? "Is your friend meeting you?"

"She's already gone home and is waiting for me there." It was a white lie, but she wanted him to think someone would miss her if she didn't arrive home.

Maybe he thought it strange that she and her friend hadn't grabbed a taxi together, but if he did, he was too polite to say so.

"Can I take your number?" he asked with a shy smile that made something in her chest clench. "I'd really love to see you again."

She nodded, heat rising to her cheeks, having to suppress a little smile of happiness. "Sure."

They exchanged numbers, and then he walked her out to the taxi rank. He made no attempt to try to get in with her—something she wasn't sure if she was disappointed or happy about—but instead leaned in and kissed her on the cheek. "It was lovely meeting you tonight, Olivia. I hope we can do it again soon." And he gave her a final smile before slamming the taxi door shut.

Liv lifted her hand in a small wave as the taxi pulled away from the stand. Michael returned the wave. She sat back around to face the front, but then glanced over her shoulder again.

He was still standing on the pavement, watching the car drive away.

TWENTY MINUTES LATER, Liv was stepping through her front door. The flat was quiet, just as she'd expected it to be. Her flatmate Tammy tended to stay away most weekends, hanging out at friends' flats or with the latest boyfriend. She usually reappeared Sunday night, having partied most of the weekend away.

Liv slipped out of the dress and kicked off her shoes. She was relieved to rid herself of the heels, and stretched out her toes, rolling the balls of her feet on the soft carpet. She threw on a vest she slept in and went to the bathroom to scrub off the remains of her makeup and brush her teeth. Her shared flat was one of those new builds that insisted on having as many bathrooms as bedrooms, even though it meant the bedrooms themselves were tiny, but it did mean she was able to have her own en-suite, while her flatmate used the main bathroom as her own. It was a little luxury, but an added privacy Liv appreciated. There was even a walk-in wardrobe which was also ridiculously tiny, but meant the agents got to boast about it on the listings.

She reached into the cabinet for a new tube of toothpaste and knocked down a small pot into the sink. The pot broke open, spilling capsules onto the porcelain.

"Shit!" A couple vanished down the plug hole before she'd managed to scoop them up again. Another couple already started to dissolve in the small pool of water gathered around the plug. "Fuck it," she swore again as she did her best to scoop them up and put the ones that weren't ruined back in the small plastic pot. She had to leave the half dissolved ones as a lost cause, but managed to retrieve the rest and put the pot back in the medicine cabinet. She'd need to get a repeat prescription, which was annoying. The doctor always acted suspiciously of her, as though she was taking too many or selling them out on the streets. She understood that he could see her medical file, and had good reason to be cautious of her, but years had passed now. At what point was she going to be allowed a clean slate?

She finished getting ready for bed then went into her room and slipped between the sheets. Her thoughts drifted to the man she'd spent the better part of the evening with. Would she hear from him again? It was hard to tell. Quite often the men she thought were the keenest were the ones who completely vanished off the radar once the night was up. She didn't want to get her hopes up only to have them dashed. A guy like him was too good for someone like her. He was way out of her league, and he'd probably get home and realise that.

As she reached out to switch off her bedside lamp, her phone buzzed.

Had a great time tonight. Hope we can repeat it again soon. Michael. X.

She studied that kiss and smiled.

Chapter Three
Four Weeks Earlier

"WHAT HAPPENED TO YOU on Friday night?" Callie asked as Olivia slipped into her seat at her desk. "Meeting some hot guy and then vanishing on us."

Liv laughed and held up her hands in defence. "We shared a bottle of wine, and talked."

Her colleague gave a cheeky smile. "And then?"

"I went home."

Callie lifted her eyebrows as though to say, *oh yeah*?

"Alone!" she protested. "I swear."

The older woman sat back in her seat. "Well, that's disappointing. I was hoping for some juicy gossip."

"Nothing exciting happened with the rest of you guys after I left?"

"No, Ellen called Ryan to come and pick her up, so she disappeared with him. Stevie and Philip vanished off somewhere together. I ended up eating a kebab at two-thirty in the morning and waking up with half of it stuck to the side of my face."

Liv laughed. "Oh, nice."

"Yeah." She grimaced. "Don't let me do tequila shots again."

Ellen arrived in the office late, flustered and frantic, and making noises about bad traffic, even though she could have just as easily caught the Tube rather than Ryan driving her.

"You heard from Mr Handsome again?" she called over to Liv, once she got settled.

Liv shook her head and wrinkled her nose. "It's only Monday. Give the guy a chance."

"Just asking! I thought after his goodnight text, he might have been eager."

"Too eager isn't good," she said, though deep down she wished he'd texted her again. Sure, she could always text him, but she didn't like to be the one to do the chasing.

Liv settled into work, catching up on emails and returning phone calls she'd missed. They'd had a couple of new listings over the weekend, and she needed to make sure the properties were all showing on the relevant websites.

A number she didn't recognise lit up on her mobile, but she answered, expecting it to be a client. "Olivia Midhurst speaking."

A male voice spoke. "Hi, Olivia, it's Michael from the other night. I hope you don't mind me calling."

She sat back in surprise, her stomach doing a flip. "Michael? No, of course not. Your number didn't come up on my phone."

"Yeah, sorry about that. I'm calling from my work phone." He paused, and she wondered what he was going to say. "Um, I know it's short notice, but I wondered if you'd like to meet for lunch? I was supposed to be meeting a client, and he's cancelled on me. I have a table booked in a restaurant around the corner from Covent Garden. It seems a shame to let the booking go to waste—you have to book several weeks in advance. But I understand if it's too short notice."

"No, no, not at all." She caught Ellen's eye across the office and pointed at the phone while mouthing 'it's him' at her. Ellen's face lit up, and she grinned and gave Liv a double thumbs up.

"What time?" she asked, smiling down the phone.

"One o'clock."

"Perfect."

He gave her the address. She wished she'd put more effort into choosing her work clothes that morning—a white shirt with a tulip skirt and heels.

Ellen came over to help her get ready, and undid a couple of the top buttons of her shirt, and rifled through her makeup bag for some red lipstick. "There. You look gorgeous. The epitome of a modern businesswoman."

"Thanks. I hope I don't scare him off."

"If a man can be scared off by a strong woman, then he's not man enough for you, anyway."

"Thanks."

She glanced over at Tony's closed office door, hoping he hadn't noticed her making the extra effort. She could always say she was going to meet a new client—someone who was interested in their agency to manage a string of investment properties, perhaps—but she didn't like lying to him. He'd done her a favour by giving her the job in the first place, and besides, there were enough lies in her life without adding more. But her boss's door remained shut, and she figured she'd get away with sneaking out, just as long as she wasn't too long.

OLIVIA WALKED INTO the restaurant, scanning the crowd. She suddenly realised she didn't know Michael's surname. She wouldn't be able to tell the hostess what name he'd booked under, other than Michael. She didn't want to end up looking silly and out of place. That imposter syndrome was coming into play all over again.

She hesitated near the doorway, frantically hoping she would spot him. She breathed out a sigh of relief as he half stood from a table near the back, his hand lifting to signal her.

The hostess approached. "Can I help you?"

"Oh, that's okay. I already spotted him."

The hostess gave her a nod and a smile and left Liv to wind her way through the busy lunchtime crowd. It was loud in the restaurant, everyone talking at once, glasses clinking, and knives and forks striking plates. Below the clamour, music played, but it was too faint for her to recognise.

Her smile widened as she approached Michael. He wore a dark suit with a tie which had threads of pink running through it for a playful splash of colour. He was just as handsome as she'd remembered, perhaps even more so. As he smiled in return and leaned in to kiss her cheek, his hand pressing into the small of her back, a waft of expensive aftershave filled her senses.

"Olivia," he said. "You look beautiful."

"Thank you. You're not so bad yourself. Are you always so smartly dressed?"

He chuckled. "I do wear clothes other than a suit, I promise. I will have to take you out one weekend when I'm allowed to be more casual."

Her heart hummed at the mention of him wanting to take her out again. They hadn't even started this date yet.

He pulled her chair out for her, and she took a seat. She wasn't used to men treating her with such old-fashioned gestures, and couldn't decide if it was sweet or made her feel awkward. Maybe a little of both.

To hide her discomfort, she picked up the menu and studied it.

"The Carpaccio of beef looks amazing," she said, thinking she didn't want to order anything too heavy for a lunch dish.

"Mmm, it does look good." He looked up at her, his dark eyes fixing on hers. He was intense, in a way she felt he was looking at her too deeply, and held eye contact for a little longer than was truly comfortable. "Don't you think we're eating too much meat now, though? It's been all over the news about how bad it is for us, and the environment. Did you know they liken eating a piece of bacon to being as bad for us as smoking a cigarette?"

She shook her head. "No, I didn't know that. How awful." She resisted adding, *I love bacon.*

He maintained eye contact. "So, you'll have the salmon instead?"

"Oh, I ... Yes, well, the salmon looks delicious as well."

He smiled, and she was relieved when he finally looked away. "Excellent." He lifted a hand and signalled over to the waitress. "Two salmon Carpaccio, and we'll need a good white wine to go with that."

"I shouldn't drink," she said. "I have to get back to work." Her job was important to her, even though being an estate agent often meant she was the butt of jokes, and she didn't want to do anything to mess it up.

"Nonsense. You can't have lunch without white wine. It's practically law." He flashed her that perfect white smile, and she found herself agreeing. One glass of wine wasn't going to hurt. She'd drink plenty of water with it, and chew some gum before she got back into the office.

The waitress returned with the bottle of wine, but just set it down with the glasses, rather than making them go through the awkward tasting routine. Michael removed the bottle from the cooler and poured them both a glass.

"To second dates," he toasted, and they clinked glasses.

"Is this our second?" she asked, tilting her head to one side as she smiled at him. "Does Saturday night count as a first date?"

"Oh, absolutely. And I hope I'll get a third and forth date, too."

His phone, which sat beside him on the table, buzzed, and he glanced down at it, a frown marking his brow, his lips pinching.

"Everything okay?" she asked.

"Yes ... Well ... Yes, it's fine."

"If you need to make a call, I don't mind."

He glanced up at her, and she could see he was anxious. Perhaps he didn't want her to think he was being rude, but then she didn't want him to think she was completely uptight. This was a lunch date in the middle of a working day. She hoped if something urgent came up, he wouldn't mind her making a call either.

"Honestly, it's fine," she encouraged. "It's work. I get it."

"Are you sure?"

She waved a hand at him. "Absolutely."

Relief relaxed his features and his shoulders dropped. "Thank you. I'll be as quick as I can."

Michael pushed back from the table and got to his feet. He gave her another apologetic smile before striding across the restaurant, already swiping the screen of his mobile phone to bring up a number before putting it to his ear.

Olivia took a sip of her wine and waited. She checked her phone, quickly scanning social media for anything exciting, and made sure she didn't have any messages of her own. She'd sneaked out of work, after all, to have this lunch date. Her boss wouldn't be too happy if he found out she'd left early to get here.

Their food arrived, the waitress slipping the plates onto the table. At least the meals were chilled, so she didn't need to worry about the food getting cold while she waited. She twisted around in her seat to see Michael pacing the street, the phone still clamped to his ear.

Should she start? She didn't have any viewings that afternoon and was only working on more paperwork. Not that she normally needed to drive, anyway. The agency had a car which the staff were able to use if one of the properties they were managing was out of the way, but mainly they either walked to the location or caught the Tube. That was the thing about working in London—most of the time it was faster and cheaper to just catch the Tube rather than sitting in traffic and going through the nightmare of trying to find somewhere to park.

She took another sip of the wine and realised she'd almost finished the glass already and she hadn't even eaten anything yet. The warm buzz of alcohol made her mind cloudy, but it didn't take away from the fact she was feeling awkward and out of place. The waitress kept glancing over, perhaps wondering if she should take the food away.

Olivia busied herself with buttering a piece of bread and taking small bites, alternating with some sips of water. She almost laughed. She was out at a fancy restaurant and was dining on bread and water.

The time ticked by both painfully slowly and equally too fast. If she didn't get back to work at a reasonable time, Tony was bound to start asking questions. She didn't want to get in trouble.

She glanced over her shoulder again, hoping to catch Michael's eye and get some indication about what she should do. If he made a gesture to tell her to start, at least she wouldn't feel as though she was being rude by eating without him, but he continued to pace, not even glancing in her direction. Her awkwardness was building to panic now, her stomach tightening, so she wasn't sure she'd even be able to eat when he did eventually come back into the restaurant. All she wanted was to be out of the situation, but indecision pinned her to the spot. She couldn't even escape to the toilet, knowing it would look strange to leave two untouched meals sitting on the table. The staff would probably think she'd left without paying.

Simply to have something to do, she picked up the bottle from the cooler and poured herself a second glass of white wine.

"Everything okay with your meals?" the waitress asked as she wandered past the table, clearly sensing something was wrong.

"Oh, yes, fine. My date's got caught up in a business call. I'm sure he'll be done soon."

Liv drank the second glass too quickly. She was feeling a little drunk now, and she picked at the fish. It looked too raw, and her stomach lurched.

There was a flash of movement near the table, and Michael slid back into the seat opposite. He immediately picked up his fork. "I am so sorry. I had no idea that was going to take so long."

"Everything all right?" she asked, hoping her words didn't come out slurred from the wine.

He grimaced. "Could be better."

He took a couple of mouthfuls of the salmon and washed it down with the wine. "You should have started without me."

"It's okay. I wasn't that hungry, anyway."

She forced herself to eat something, but her anxiety had taken hold now.

"I hate to do this to you," he said, "but I'm going to have to take off. I've got some stuff back at the office I need to deal with."

"Oh, right." Her fuzzy brain told her she should be having more of a reaction, but she couldn't quite muster the energy.

"Let me make it up to you, one evening this week. No work phone calls, I promise."

Olivia forced a smile. "Sure, that would be lovely."

She went to stand up with him, but he put his hand out. "Stay where you are. Finish your meal." He slid some notes under a saucer. "That should be plenty to cover the bill."

"I can pay for my own meal," she protested.

"Not at all. I wouldn't hear of it."

He leaned in again and kissed her cheek. "I really am terribly sorry about this, Olivia. I feel wretched."

"It's fine," she said again, only wanting him to leave now, so she could escape as well. She'd gone from feeling excited and nervous, to being slightly drunk and deflated. She only wanted to go and hide somewhere no one would be able to look at her.

"I'll call you, then."

"Great."

She watched as he turned and left. The moment he'd vanished from the restaurant and turned the corner, she bent to gather her bag. Wooziness washed over her, and she straightened again, clutching the edge of the table to steady herself, the tablecloth white and starched beneath her fingertips.

"Everything okay?" the waitress asked her, and Olivia looked up to see her standing in front of her, a concerned expression on her young features.

"Oh, yes, fine. Something came up." She pushed the notes Michael had left across the table toward her. "Keep the change."

Liv got to her feet and hurried from the restaurant.

Chapter Four
Four Weeks Earlier

SHE DIDN'T KNOW WHY, but she didn't want to tell everyone at work what had happened during the date.

No, she knew why she was reluctant to say anything. They'd tell her Michael had been out of order to leave her sitting alone for so long, and she shouldn't see him again. Perhaps she shouldn't, but he hadn't been able to help it. He'd apologised and offered to make it up to her. Still, that didn't change how he'd made her feel by leaving her sitting on her own the entire time.

Did she even want to see him again? It had been a long time since someone of his calibre had been interested in her, and she knew nothing about his job—it could have been something seriously important. The situation had been far from ideal, but was it worth writing him off just because he had to make a phone call?

"Are you okay?" Ellen asked her that afternoon as she sat at her desk, trying to focus on the mountain of paperwork that seemed to have doubled in size since the morning. "You seem a little quiet."

"Just tired. I had a glass of wine too many over lunch."

Ellen gave her a wink. "He was worth it though, right?

"Absolutely," she agreed.

Ellen wedged her backside onto the edge of Liv's desk and folded her arms. "So, when are you seeing him again—assuming you *are* seeing him again?"

She gave a small smile and glanced away, as though suddenly interested in the stack of references she'd been going through. "He's going to take me out for dinner one evening. He said he'll call to arrange it."

"This week? Wow, he's keen."

"Yeah, I guess." Liv didn't fill her in on how this was an apology dinner to make up for the disastrous lunch date. "Anyway, I really need to get on with this, especially after taking the extended lunch break."

Ellen held both hands up and straightened. "All right, Miss Conscientious. I'll let you get on. Tell me if you hear anything else, though."

Luckily, her boss Tony hadn't noticed her gone for so long, so she drank a strong coffee and tried to focus on work instead of men.

The afternoon dragged by, and she checked her phone too many times, wondering if Michael would send another text to say sorry, but there was nothing. He was busy, and she needed to stop caring so much. She didn't even know the guy, but he seemed to have wound his way into her thoughts. Why was that? She didn't normally let a man affect her in such a way. Normally, she was content with a one night stand and never needing to see the man again. Getting involved with someone meant too many questions she couldn't answer, and she'd learned from experience that things got complicated. Far easier to get what she wanted in the bedroom and not even bother to exchange phone numbers. She'd discovered most men were quite happy for things to go that way as well.

But not this one. Something was different about him.

A HEADACHE HAD BEEN building all afternoon, lodging right behind her eyes and thumping with resilience. Several large glasses of water and a couple of pain killers had done nothing to shift it, and now Liv only wanted to lie down and sleep for the rest of the evening.

She pushed open the door to her flat to discover her flatmate Tammy slamming around. Liv's heart sank.

"Everything okay?" she called tentatively.

"Why does this fucking flat have to be such a mess all the time? I leave it perfectly fine on Friday morning, and by Monday it's a fucking tip again." Tammy picked up one perfectly positioned cushion and slammed it back down in exactly the same place.

There hadn't been anything wrong with the state of the flat when she'd left first thing that morning, so unless someone had broken in during the day and made a mess of the place, she figured Tammy was overreacting.

"It's fine, Tammy. There's nothing wrong with the flat."

"Only because I've been back here for the last hour cleaning up. There were dishes in the sink, and I bet you haven't hoovered all weekend."

The 'dishes' she was referring to were that morning's cereal bowl and a mug which she'd drunk her tea from. She'd been running late, and so had simply rinsed them and left them in the sink to finish later. She should have known it would cause a fuss.

"It was one bowl and one cup, Tammy. And actually, I did whip around with the hoover on Saturday morning."

"That's two days ago!"

She didn't have the patience for this. "Not everyone vacuums every day. If you want to, you should be here to do it."

"I'm not making the mess!"

She gritted her teeth, doing her best to keep her temper. "There is no mess. You go out partying every weekend, and then come back on a downer and wanting to pick a fight. The flat is perfectly tidy. Now, I have a stinking headache, so I'm going to lie down, in my room, in my mess."

She turned her back on Tamsin and went straight to her room, shutting the door behind her. Tammy was normally fine, except for on a Monday. Too many recreational drugs Friday to Sunday made her OCD tendencies flare up, and she liked to take it out on Olivia.

The roar of the vacuum cleaner sounded outside her door, and she knew Tammy was doing it deliberately. Liv gave a growl of frustration, threw herself on her bed, and picked up her pillow. She jammed it over her head to try to block out the noise. If Tammy was going to continue like this, Olivia was going to find somewhere else to live. Change always made her nervous, thinking they'd ask for too many references and check too far back in her history, but she'd end up killing her flatmate if this continued for much longer.

ANOTHER DAY PASSED, and she didn't hear from Michael. She told herself it was a good thing. She didn't need some workaholic man in her life, and it wasn't as though she'd had fun the last time she'd seen him—quite the opposite. Yet she still found herself checking her phone more than normal, and her heart raced each time she had a message, and then plummeted again when it wasn't from him. Ellen and Callie had both enquired into whether or not he'd called again, but after a couple more times of telling them he hadn't, they stopped asking.

She was getting ready for work, her hair still wet and wrapped up in a towel turban as she flicked through the clothes in her tiny walk-in wardrobe. She took care of the things she owned, knowing that appearing well put together was one of the things that stopped people asking too many questions about her.

The ringing of her mobile phone snatched her attention from what she was doing, and her stomach lurched. No one ever called. Everyone she knew sent text messages if they wanted to get in touch. Leaving the wardrobe, she went back into the bedroom to where her phone was lying face up on her bed.

The name 'Michael' flashed up on screen. It was him.

She hesitated. Maybe she should make him wait? He hadn't even sent her a text since their disastrous date, but then she hadn't texted him either, and she didn't want to play games. Not wanting it to go to answer phone, she snatched up her mobile and swiped to answer.

"Michael, hi."

She heard him take a breath on the other end of the line. "Hi, Liv. It's good to hear your voice. I was almost surprised you answered."

"You were?" she said, trying to play innocent. "Why?"

"Because I left you in such a rush on Monday. I'd half convinced myself you wouldn't want to see me again."

"Oh, it was no big deal. I thought I said that." She winced at her own lie. Why did she feel the need to do that?

"I know, but even so. If the situation had been reversed, I don't think I'd have bothered to answer."

She didn't know how to take that. Was he saying he thought she was more forgiving than he was, or that he thought enough of himself to not waste time on someone who abandoned their date in the middle of a meal?

He must have picked up on her silence. "Anyway, let me make it up to you. Are you free tonight?"

She was tempted to say she was busy, just to judge his reaction, but she did want to see him. Perhaps she was being too hard on him. He did sound like he wanted to make up for the crappy lunch.

"Tonight would be great."

Chapter Five
Present Day

THE MAN WAS DEFINITELY waking up.

His arms and legs twitched, and his chin lifted from his chest a couple of inches before dropping back down. He let out a moan, but the gag forced between his lips muffled the sound.

She lived in fear of him working the gag free, but for the moment it was tied so tight around the back of his head, the material cut into the sides of his mouth. It wasn't going anywhere. But she still needed answers from him, and there was only one other way of getting them, and that involved untying one of his hands. It would be dangerous, but not as dangerous as if she let him speak.

Her heart thrummed, beating hard against her rib cage. She needed to keep control of her emotions. If he saw weakness in her, he'd figure out how to use it against her. He'd already done that once, and she wasn't going to make the same mistake twice.

She was ever conscious of time running out. How much did she have left? She wasn't sure, but with every minute that ticked by, the possibility that the worst might have happened filled her. He was the only one who knew the truth, and she couldn't let him continue to sleep. He needed to wake up.

On the floor, at her feet, was a plastic bottle of water. She'd brought it down here for herself, knowing this was going to make her thirsty. He was a big man, and though she was tall, she wasn't exactly muscular. It had taken a lot of effort to get him into a position where he'd been half slung over her shoulder, and then she'd had to push upward and use her other hand to pull his hands up and tie them to the hook hanging from the ceiling. It had been awkward and physically hard. Ideally, she could have done with another person to help her, but that was impossible. Her muscles had been screaming in protest by the time she'd managed to get the first hand tied. Her whole body had trembled beneath his with the exertion, and she knew she'd feel the strain for days to come—should she live that long. At least once she'd done that, she'd been able to take her shoulder away and let him dangle by that one arm while she'd tied the second one up. It must have been horribly painful—that one shoulder joint taking all of the strain—but he'd been unconscious, and besides, he deserved the pain. After everything he'd done, he deserved far more than an aching arm. By the time this was over, she thought there was a good chance he'd have paid for at least a tiny amount of what he'd put everyone else through. He deserved everything he got.

A thin trickle of blood ran from his hairline and down the side of his face. A small thrill went through her at the sight of the blood, which was immediately followed by a wave of nausea. She didn't want to take any pleasure in this—not at all. This was a necessity, not something she was enjoying doing. But when she thought of all the others he had hurt, it was difficult not to experience that stab of bitterness. Life might not have been perfect before he'd walked into it, but it had been normal—or at least as normal as her life had ever been—and now everything was one big fucking mess.

But no, she was going to put things right again. Maybe not everything would be able to go back to how it had been, but she needed to do what she could.

Stooping down, she snatched up the bottle of water at her feet and unscrewed the lid. Her pulse tripped as she stepped forward, her fingers tight around the plastic bottle, her knuckles white. Even taking the extra step closer to him sent her entire body into overdrive. Every part of her screamed, 'run, danger', but she forced her feet to plant on the concrete floor. Forced herself to stay. She wasn't doing this for herself. She needed to be brave.

With a swing of her hand, she threw some of the contents of the bottle into his face.

The result was instantaneous. The man jolted awake, his head jerking up. He sucked in a long breath through the material of the gag, as though he'd been held underwater and was only now coming up for air.

The bottle of water slipped from her fingers and hit the floor. It fell to the side, the remaining water inside glugging out of the neck and onto the concrete floor.

She wanted to stand tall and be brave, but she found herself scurrying backwards, sick with nerves. She shouldn't be frightened of him. He was the one tied up and gagged, but she couldn't help it. Knowing everything he'd done was enough to make her terrified, and she hated that she felt as though she couldn't trust herself around him. But maybe she was stronger than she'd given herself credit for. Others hadn't been able to resist him, but she had. Even after everything he'd said, she hadn't done what he'd wanted. Almost, but not quite.

"I don't want to have to hurt you, but unless you tell me what you did, you're not leaving me with any choice."

He growled behind the gag and shook his head furiously. She didn't want to meet his eye, worried he'd be able to affect her actions somehow. She could read the rage within their depths, and the thoughts going through his head. He'd kill her if he got free, she didn't doubt it, but she didn't intend on letting him go any time soon.

"Tell me," she demanded again, forcing herself to get a hold of her fear.

He snarled again, his upper lip curled around the gag. Where before he'd seemed kind of out of it, now his fierce intelligence was back, glinting in his eyes, and that made him all the more dangerous. It didn't appear as though he was going to have a change of heart, however.

Was a little part of her relieved about that? She didn't like the mixed emotions it sent through her, but she couldn't help it. The idea of releasing one of his hands terrified her, but it was the only way. She couldn't risk removing the gag. Though she needed information, time was running out, but at least the moment when he'd have a hand free wasn't coming just yet.

She crossed the space to where she'd left the cane propped against the wall. She reached down and picked it up. It was lighter than it looked, and she couldn't help sweeping it through the air, liking the whistling noise the movement made.

She turned to look at the man again. His gaze flicked down to the cane, his eyes widening. His back must still be stinging from the strikes she'd given him earlier, and receiving a second round of whippings would hurt even more. But she needed to break the dark defiance in his eyes. Just getting his admission wouldn't be enough. Even if he nodded to say he'd give her what she needed, she still wouldn't be able to risk untying that hand. She had to see he was broken and he'd tell her everything instead of trying to fight back.

It wasn't in her to be violent, but she made herself picture what he'd done and used that to push her hand. She circled him, knowing she'd find this easier if she wasn't able to look into his eyes. Standing behind him removed his face from view.

With muscles bunched and teeth gritted, she lifted the hand holding the cane and brought it down with a crack across his naked back.

Through the gag, the man screamed.

Chapter Six
Four Weeks Earlier

OLIVIA WAS DUE TO MEET Michael in less than thirty minutes, and she hadn't managed to leave the flat yet. She was on her fourth change of outfits, and still couldn't decide. Everything she tried on was either too dressy or too casual, and she couldn't find a happy medium.

She took a large gulp of the gin and tonic she'd poured herself to settle her nerves.

With a growl of frustration, she went back to her first outfit—fitted jeans, with a top in emerald green that complimented her red hair and pale skin, and a pair of silver heels. She shook her hair loose and downed the remainder of her drink. She would have to do.

Liv left her bedroom, passing through the open plan living area to reach the front door.

Tamsin sat on the couch and craned her neck to take in the sight of Liv as she passed by. "Ooh, hot date?" she called in a sing-song voice.

Liv still hadn't quite forgiven her for Monday's dramatics. "Yep, scorching."

"Don't do anything I wouldn't do!"

She didn't know exactly what it was Tammy *wouldn't* do. From the wild stories she came back with after her weekends spent partying, Liv figured it wasn't much.

"See you later," she said, pulling open the front door.

"Don't make too much noise if you get in late. I can never get back to sleep if you wake me."

Liv gave a growl of annoyance under her breath and yanked the front door shut behind her, deliberately giving it an extra slam. Bloody Tammy. She wasn't going to let her annoying flatmate ruin her mood. She was excited to see Michael again, and the gin and tonic she'd drunk had put a bounce in her step.

She should have caught the Tube into the city, but instead she grabbed a taxi, knowing how late she was running. It wouldn't do him any harm to wait, especially after the other day, but she didn't want him to give up on her either.

LIV PUSHED HER WAY into the crowded, noisy bar, immediately casting her gaze across all the people, trying to spot him. Within seconds, she did. He was leaning against the bar, casually dressed in jeans and a shirt, with the sleeves rolled up to reveal a pair of attractive forearms. She was glad she'd gone for jeans as well now. It had been the right choice. Nerves churned in her stomach and her heart raced, and she already felt overheated and sweaty from the adrenaline. Pushing down her anxiety, she lifted her chin and did her best to appear confident.

"Hey," he said as she approached. He flashed a wide smile full of straight, white teeth. "I was starting to worry you'd stand me up as a punishment."

She laughed. "No, not at all. If I was going to punish you, you'd know about it." She gave him a wink, and then cringed inside. Why the hell had she said that?

He didn't seem to mind. "I'll look forward to that. What can I get you to drink?"

She ordered another gin and tonic, and he made it a double. She opened her mouth to tell him a single was fine, but the bartender had already turned away to the optics at the back of the bar. She'd already had the drink at home, so she'd have to make sure she sipped this one. It was easy to drink too much when she was nervous.

Michael paid for their drinks. He had a bottle of beer and was drinking straight from the neck. He seemed relaxed and carefree, unlike the man she'd watched pace back and forth outside of the restaurant the other day. She needed to figure out how to relax as well, but being relaxed wasn't her usual state.

They found a table in the corner where the music wasn't as loud, and took seats opposite each other.

He leaned in towards her. "I really am sorry about the other day. It's been playing on my mind ever since."

She shook her head. "Please, stop apologising. We'll start again fresh from today, yeah?"

He grinned and lifted his beer bottle up in a salute. "To fresh starts."

Liv returned the smile and raised her glass to clink against the bottle. "So, are we going to have a toast at the start of every date?"

He chuckled. "I don't see why not. It could be the start of a fun tradition."

She hid her smile this time, a rush of warm pleasure flooding through her veins. "I like traditions."

She caught his eye, and they stared at each other across the table, both of them understanding what that meant. Traditions were something developed over time, and if they were talking about traditions, it meant they were contemplating this being more than just a fling.

Michael was the first to glance away, but he quickly pulled his gaze back to hers. "You said you're an estate agent?"

She nodded. "Yes, that's right."

"So, you're used to office situations and how awkward they can get."

"Umm, I suppose so." She wondered where this was going.

He sighed and sat back in his seat. "Can I confide in you about something?"

His mood had grown serious, and she sat forward in her seat. "Of course."

"It has to do with the reason I was so distracted during lunch the other day. I have a work colleague—a friend, really—who I've worked with for years, and first thing Monday morning, I walked into his office to find him in a somewhat personal position with a woman who isn't his wife."

She widened her eyes. "Oh, my God."

"The person he was bending over his desk was his secretary, and we have a strict no fraternizing with the staff policy. So, he's put me in a very difficult situation, not only of feeling like I'm lying to his wife when I see her, but also covering up for him breaking company policy on relationships."

"That is a difficult position to be in."

He leaned toward her, reducing the distance between them. "What would you do if you were me?"

She considered everything for a moment. "If it comes out that you already knew and didn't do anything, would it cause you problems at work?"

He nodded. "Yes, of course."

"Then you need to tell your friend that he needs to go to HR and own up himself, and tell them the relationship with the secretary is over. What he tells his wife is between him and his wife, but if it's going to affect you at work, that's something he needs to take ownership of."

Michael sighed and raked his fingers through his thick, dark hair. The action stirred something inside her. "Yes, you're right. That's what I was on the phone about the other day—he was trying to convince me to stay quiet."

"And you have so far?"

"Yes, I have, but it's eating away at me. If he was angry and threatening, I'd go to HR right away, but he seems so genuinely distressed by the whole thing."

She took another sip of her drink and thought, *not as distressed as his wife would be*, but managed to keep her mouth shut.

Michael continued. "He begged and pleaded with me not to say anything, and promised me it's over with the secretary, but they're together for eight hours a day, five days a week. I can't see how it can really be over when you spend that much time in the proximity of the person you've been having sex with."

She went to take another sip of her drink and discovered the glass empty. He noticed and pointed casually with one finger. "Can I get you another?"

"Sure."

Liv relaxed into the date, feeling more comfortable now that he'd shared something that was going on in his life, especially as it had explained what had happened during their lunch date. When Michael got up to use the bathroom or go to the bar for more drinks, she noticed how other women watched him as he moved through the room, and pride swelled within her when he sat back down opposite her. The more time she was spending with him, the more she realised how lonely she had been. It was fine to have one night stands, but they'd left her feeling low and empty. She had Ellen and Callie at work, but they had their own lives, too.

Now, sitting opposite this gorgeous, attentive man who was hanging on her every word, she found herself starting to wonder if she could actually have someone for herself.

Chapter Seven
Four Weeks Earlier

OLIVIA EDGED OPEN HER eyes. Her mouth tasted as though something had died in it while she slept, and her temples pounded. The familiar contents of her bedside table and the chest of drawers on the wall adjacent to her bed slowly began to take shape. She was relieved to discover she was in her own bed. At least she'd made it home last night, though she had no idea how she'd managed it.

A sudden dart of panic shot through her, and she froze. Was she alone? She'd been out on a date with Michael, and the last thing she really remembered was walking along the street, arm-in-arm with him, giggling about something. Had they come back here, and something happened between them? Was he in bed beside her? Lifting her throbbing head cautiously from the pillow, ignoring the little puddle of dribble she'd left on the material, she twisted her head and peered over her shoulder.

Liv exhaled a sigh of relief and dropped back down into the bed. She didn't know what had happened, but she was definitely alone. She would have hated for her first time with Michael to be some drunken romp she couldn't even remember. Ugh.

What must he think of her? Had he drunk as much as she had, or had he been sober and she'd just made a complete idiot out of herself? She was normally so conservative with the amount she drank, but the double shots of gin, together with getting too comfortable with Michael, obviously had meant she'd got carried away.

She reached down beside the bed and scrambled around for her phone. Checking the screen, she hoped to see a message from him, perhaps something sweet and funny to put her mind at rest, but the screen was blank. Her stomach swirled nauseatingly, but it wasn't just the effects of the alcohol—though she didn't think she'd even drunk that much, a gin and tonic at home, and a couple more at the bar when they'd met. She must have had a ton more afterwards to not even remember getting home.

No, the uncomfortable feeling wasn't from the alcohol—it was from not being able to remember. She'd had blackouts before, but not for a long time. That had been a dark point in her life, something she thought she'd left behind. The last thing she wanted was to return there. She'd done everything she could to put that side of her behind her.

With her phone still in her hand, she tapped out a quick message to Michael.

Thanks for getting me home last night. Sorry if I did anything embarrassing! Too many G&Ts. X

He might not even reply. If she'd made a complete fool of herself, he probably wouldn't want to see her again. He was a reserved kind of guy, not the sort who would want some drunk woman on his arm.

She groaned and covered her face with her hands. She needed water and painkillers, and then some more sleep.

Oh, shit.

She sat up, her stomach lurching. It was Thursday today, and she was supposed to be working. Snatching up her phone again, she checked the time. Quarter to nine. She was supposed to be in the office in fifteen minutes.

Well, that was never going to happen.

Guilt swamped over her as she swiped the phone for the number for her office. She put on her best croaky voice, which wasn't too hard considering how dehydrated she was.

Callie picked up the phone. "Blue Scene Agents," she chirped down the line.

"Callie, it's Olivia. Could you put me through to Tony?"

"Yeah, of course Olivia. Are you okay? You sound horrible."

Her guilt intensified. "No, not really. I've picked up a bout of food poisoning, or possibly even Norovirus. I'm not sure which, but it isn't pretty. You guys definitely don't want me in today."

"Oh, no. That sounds horrible. Please, stay away. No offence."

She managed a smile, though Callie couldn't see it. "None taken."

"Okay, I can see him in his office. It looks like he's free. I'm putting you through now. Feel better soon!"

"Thanks."

The phone beeped a couple of times and then her boss picked up. "Good morning, Olivia. Callie says you're not well."

"Yeah, I'm so sorry to let you down, but there's no way I can come in today, not unless you want me infecting the entire team."

"Oh, God, no. That's the last thing we want. Take tomorrow, too, if you need it and come back in healthy on Monday. I know how these things can spread."

"Thanks, Tony. I appreciate it. I do have my laptop here, so if anything urgent comes up, just shoot me an email."

"I'm sure we can survive a couple of days without you, Olivia, but thanks for the offer."

"Sure."

The phone buzzed against her ear, indicating a message had come through, but she couldn't check it while she was still on the phone with her boss.

On the end of the line, Tony hesitated as though he wasn't sure what else to say. "Well, plenty of water and dehydration salts," he finished, "and we'll see you Monday."

"Okay, bye."

Relieved, she hung up. She hoped he hadn't noticed the long lunch she'd taken on Monday as well. The last thing she wanted was for her career to go down the pan. It was the one part of her life she thought she was doing well at.

Her stomach twisted, wrung out. She remembered the message and checked the screen. Michael had replied.

Not at all! You were fine when you got in the taxi. Had a wonderful evening. Looking forward to seeing you again soon. X

Olivia frowned at the message. He must just be being polite. How could she possibly have been fine when she felt this bad the next day and couldn't even remember getting in the taxi, never mind coming home? Had she gone somewhere else after getting in the taxi and drunk some more? No, she wouldn't have done that, she was sure. Well, almost sure. She couldn't remember, so she couldn't be completely certain of anything. The most rational explanation was simply that Michael was being polite, or perhaps he hadn't even noticed how drunk she was. She wished she could remember getting in the taxi; at least then she'd have an idea of how much she drunk before that. It was the not knowing that was the frustrating part. But at least he'd messaged her back and said he wanted to see her again, so she figured she hadn't done anything too bad.

Olivia reached to her bedside table and picked up the glass of water sitting there. She drank the entire thing down in several gulps, the liquid sitting loose and uneasy in her belly. She stared at the empty glass. Had she managed to get herself some fresh water when she'd come in, or had someone else poured the glass of water for her? Her thoughts went to her flatmate. Perhaps Tammy had seen her come home last night. She'd warned Liv not to wake her up, but if Tammy had seen her arrive in a drunken mess, she might have put her to bed. Olivia might have said or done something that would give her an idea of what had happened.

Quickly, she swiped her phone on again and sent out a message to Tamsin. The other woman would be at work now, but she always had her phone on her.

Hi. Did you hear me come in last night? Sorry if I woke you.

The reply came back almost immediately.

Nope. Slept like a log. Take it you had a good night then! See you later.

Olivia didn't know which other way to turn. What about her medication? Had she forgotten to take her pills, or perhaps had taken too many? She thought she had a pretty good balance now and was on an even keel. Perhaps the extra drink had reacted badly with the meds. Strictly speaking, she wasn't even supposed to drink, but a couple was normally fine. She'd have to be more careful in the future.

She crawled out of bed and took a quick shower and brushed her teeth to try to make herself feel more human, then put her pyjamas and dressing gown back on. She had no intention of going anywhere today, and anyway, she was supposed to be sick, and the last thing she needed was someone spotting her and reporting back to her boss. In the kitchen, she made tea in the largest mug she could find, and managed to get some toast and marmalade inside her to settle her stomach.

She intended on spending the rest of the day dozing and watching Netflix, and trying not to think about what might have happened the night before.

Chapter Eight
Three Weeks Earlier

OLIVIA DID AS TONY suggested and took the Friday off as well. By Saturday morning, she was bored out of her mind and starting to go stir-crazy in the flat by herself.

The morning had dawned with one of those surprisingly bright and warm spring days that made London feel like a whole different place. She wanted to go somewhere with a picnic blanket and a good book, lie in the sun for the day, and forget about everything else. The missing hours from the other night still hadn't returned, and, despite saying he'd wanted to see her again soon in his text message, she hadn't heard from Michael either. His silence made her think there was more to the missing hours than he'd let on, and she'd probably said or done something that made him not want to see her again. She didn't blame him. She'd thought he was out of her league right from the start.

Tammy had done her usual disappearing act for the weekend right after she'd finished work on Friday night, and Ellen was with Ryan, doing loved-up, couple things.

Loneliness swept over her. Was there anyone else she could call—one of the other girls from the office, perhaps? But considering she was supposed to have some kind of contagious vomiting bug, she didn't think anyone would be too pleased to hear from her.

Suck it up, Livvy, she told herself. *You are completely content with your own company. You don't need anyone else.*

She'd take herself down to Hyde Park and find a spot by the serpentine to hang out. There was no reason she couldn't have a lovely day on her own.

With her mind made up, she gathered her things. She'd checked her handbag to see if it contained any clues as to what had happened the other night, but there wasn't even as much as a receipt from the taxi driver. Why would there be? The only time she got receipts from drivers was if it had to do with work and she needed to claim it back on expenses.

Olivia left her flat and caught the Tube the handful of stops to Lancaster Gate. The Tube was loud and busy, and she hung onto a pole while the train rocked and swayed through the tunnels. The musty stink of body odour filled her nostrils, and she turned her face to press her nose into her shoulder and tried not to think how many sweaty hands had held the pole before her.

She exited the station into the fresh air and sunshine and walked the short distance to the park. It seemed half of London had decided to do the same thing, with groups of young people and families occupying almost every spot of grass. The teenagers wore too little clothing—the boys shirtless and the girls in summer dresses or shorts with their t-shirts rolled up under their bras to create belly-tops, exposing inches of flat, flawless skin.

Liv found a spot in the shade, aware that as much as she loved the sun, it only made her freckles blend together, rather than gave her an actual tan, and tried not to feel jealous of all the youngsters with their easy lives and company. She'd brought a paperback and a cold drink. Though she opened the book and tried to read, she found her gaze drawn to those around her rather than the story. She wondered about all their different lives, what their relationships were with each other. The couple walking side by side, but not touching—were they actually a couple, or just friends, or perhaps it was an illicit relationship, like the one Michael had been talking about, the boss and the secretary, and they simply didn't want anyone else to see them holding hands?

She people watched for a while, picking at daisies absentmindly. A tiny ladybird crawled its way up her leg, and she let it continue, its tiny legs tickling her skin, before she gently gave the insect a nudge with her finger and it spread its wings and took off into the spring sunshine. *Fly away home. Your house is on fire and your children are gone.* What was it with all these nursery rhymes being so sadistic?

The boredom she'd been experiencing at home hadn't abated now that she was out and about. It was company she was missing more than anything else.

She got to her feet, brushed down her backside for any dried grass clinging to her, and folded up the blanket she'd been sitting on. She'd take a walk, browse some shops, maybe. Anything to while away the time. A cold beer with lunch tempted her, but she'd managed to stay away from alcohol since the other night, and she didn't want to risk one beer turning into a couple. She'd be trying to drink away the boredom, and it had been the drink that had created this issue in the first place.

Olivia strolled through the park, staying beneath the shade cast by the huge oak trees bordering the path. She took the exit that would take her towards Hyde Park Corner and wandered out of the park and down onto the adjacent street. This was tourist central now, and the various carts lining the pavement catered for them all.

A little cart sold ice cream, while another peddled handmade jewellery. One particular stand clearly catered for the tourists, with the Union Jack plastered across mugs, and small teddy bears, and t-shirts.

She stopped short, her breath catching.

He stood side-on, so she was easily able to make out his profile. The straight nose, and full mouth, and strong jaw. But his lips were pinched, his normally smooth brow furrowed. He was pointing, leaning forward almost aggressively.

Michael.

Liv switched her line of sight to the person he was pointing at, and her stomach dropped. A pretty blonde woman, petite in stature. She held her hands out on both sides of her body as a gesture of exasperation, and then flicked one of her hands towards him. He said something else in return then shook his head and stormed away. The young woman watched him go before shaking her head herself and turning and disappearing into the throng of tourists and Saturday shoppers.

Olivia hesitated. What had that been all about? Was he dating someone else and she'd just witnessed a lovers' tiff? She didn't have any reason to be jealous, but she couldn't help the bitterness rising up inside her. It wasn't as though they were anywhere near being exclusive to one another. Hell, they'd only had a couple of dates, and neither of them had gone wonderfully well, that she could remember, anyway. Yet something about him intrigued her, and without even thinking, she found herself hurrying down the road after him. She didn't know what she'd say when she reached him, if she even would speak to him. Maybe she'd just follow him for a little while and see where he ended up.

But he must have sensed her, as he glanced over his shoulder. Perhaps he hadn't sensed her at all, but instead had been looking to see if the blonde had followed him. Either way, he locked eyes with Liv, and her heart jolted in her chest.

Michael frowned and came to an abrupt halt. He spun to face her.

"Olivia?"

She stopped short as well, blinking in surprise, trying to act as though she hadn't known it was him. "Oh, my gosh, Michael. What are you doing here?"

"I was about to ask the same of you."

She lifted the picnic blanket and bag containing her book. "I wanted to make the most of the sunshine, so I've been reading in the park. I wandered down this way to look for somewhere for lunch." She kicked herself for mentioning lunch. She hoped he wouldn't think she was hinting for him to take her out again. "What about you?" she added, trying to turn the topic around.

"Oh, I was doing a little shopping. It was going well until I was short-changed by one of the stall holders." He motioned up the road to where she'd seen him arguing. Something inside her relaxed.

"Oh no, that's a shame. What did you buy?"

"Sorry?"

"You said you were short-changed. I wondered what you'd bought."

He flapped a hand at her. "Oh, nothing in the end. I told her to keep it."

Liv frowned. "You did? So she got your money and you walked away with nothing."

"I know. Stupid of me. But I was so angry. I didn't want anything from her anymore."

"Really?"

He gave a laugh, but it sounded forced. "I know. Not my smartest move, cutting my nose off to spite my face. Anyway, I've been meaning to call you. What are you doing now?"

"Oh, not much."

"You mentioned lunch. I'm kind of peckish myself. You want to grab something together?"

Tell him no, a little voice that sounded suspiciously like Ellen's hissed in her head. He hadn't called her, and his story about why he'd been arguing with the blonde didn't feel right. Besides, the last couple of times when she'd been out with him hadn't exactly gone well, or at least, in the case of their last date, she couldn't remember if it had or not.

He must have sensed her reluctance and reached down and took her hand. His dark eyes had a way of pulling her in, making the world around her fade into background noise. "I really would love to spend some more time with you, Liv."

She been lonely all morning, and the idea of not only company, but handsome male company made her give in. "Sure, that would be great."

She glanced over her shoulder, trying to make out the blonde working at one of the stalls. His story felt off, but why would he lie?

"There's a lovely bistro about ten minutes from here. It has an outside area so we can sit in the sun."

"As long as there's a parasol. My complexion doesn't do well with direct sunlight."

He looked at her. "You have a beautiful complexion. Really. Just like the rest of you."

His compliment made her blush, and she pushed the image of him fighting with the blonde out of her head.

LUNCH WAS A SMORGASBORD of different breads and olives, with pesto drizzled mozzarella balls and ripe tomatoes. As promised, they had a table outside, with a parasol to offer Liv some shade. She washed the food down with an ice-cold beer, and the conversation flowed. Liv discovered Michael, like her, was an only child, and they regaled stories of childhood, how they'd both always stared in fascination at their friends with siblings, wondering how those relationships worked, and envying them so deeply for their easy ability to seemingly love and hate each other at the same time. He entertained her with tales that made her laugh, of a time when he'd stolen a microphone from a karaoke bar and kept singing in the taxi the whole way home, much to the chagrin of the driver.

It didn't take long for her to forget all about the blonde and the lack of purchase he'd apparently been short changed for.

With lunch finished, they left the bistro and stepped out onto the street, both uncertain of what was to come next. There was an unspoken potential between them, a possibility that neither wanted to give voice to. The street was busy with tourists, and the sun bore down on them, heating the pavement below their feet, so it felt as though they were blasted with heat from both directions. They were standing face to face, only a couple of inches between their bodies.

Michael reached down and brushed a free strand of hair from her face, the backs of his knuckles grazing her jaw, the contact sending sparks through her body. His fingers caught hers and he tugged her closer, so their bodies met.

Her breath caught, her heart racing. He was going to kiss her.

She lifted her chin, and he ducked his head, pausing only a fraction from her mouth. He was giving her the opportunity to meet him the rest of the way, showing him it was what she wanted. It was. Their lips met, and his were soft, warm, and firm, and she opened her mouth so their tongues touched. That familiar surge of desire soared up inside her, and she felt his urgency, too. His hand dropped hers and slipped around to the small of her back, pulling her closer. She pressed her body up against his, only partly aware they were making out like a couple of teenagers in the middle of the street.

She broke the kiss. "We should go back to mine. My flatmate won't be there." Her voice was breathy, flustered.

He nodded, and she noted the high flush in his cheeks, and how kissable his lips looked. "Yes, let's do that."

They both knew what that meant. They'd taken a step on an inevitable path now, but Olivia could see no point in getting off. This was a handsome, professional man, who genuinely seemed to like her. They were both adults. She wracked her mind, trying to remember if she had any condoms at her place. Yes, she did. She'd bought some a few months back—not that she'd had the opportunity to use them.

"My flat is only a few tube stops from here."

"Screw that." He lifted a hand to signal a passing cab. "We'll get a taxi."

Within minutes, they were settled in the back seat of a cab, with Liv giving the driver her address. They kissed again, Michael's hand sliding up her thigh. She'd only worn a summer dress that morning because of the gorgeous weather, and it didn't offer much coverage. Not that she minded and, by the way his hand slid higher and higher up the outside of her thigh to her hip and the elastic of her underwear, neither did Michael.

They pulled up outside her building, and Michael threw money at the driver before climbing out and pulling Olivia with him. She felt wild and wanton, leading this gorgeous man towards the front door of her building, knowing what would happen when they stepped inside. Holding her hand, he pulled her towards the single lift that accessed the upper floors where her flat was located, but she pulled back on him.

"No, let's take the stairs."

He glanced over his shoulder at her with a frown. "Why? Is it broken?"

"No, but I don't like lifts. I always imagine that I'm going to get stuck in them."

He grinned. "Getting stuck in a lift with me wouldn't be such a bad thing."

Even the promise of lift sex wasn't going to get her inside.

"Maybe not, but either we take the stairs, or I don't go up. It's only two floors." The building that occupied her flat and fifteen more identical ones had been built on the site of an old petrol station just a couple of roads away from Shepherd's Bush high street. Because it was a new build, it had all the mod-cons, even if the flats themselves were tiny.

"Looks like we're taking the stairs, then."

They hurried up them together and stumbled through the door, Liv managing to slam it shut behind them. Then he was kissing her again, harder this time, forceful. The tentativeness he'd shown on the street had vanished, and he shoved her against the wall beside the front door, his hand pushing up under her dress, reaching for her knickers. His other hand palmed her breast over the top of her clothing, squeezing hard so she gasped at the pain.

"Oh!"

But still he was kissing her, his tongue pushing into her mouth. He'd flattened her to the wall and she could feel his desire for her digging hard into her stomach. It was happening fast, but she was no prude, and it wasn't as though she was some innocent virgin. It felt good to be wanted, and so she met him with her own passion, pulling up his t-shirt to reveal a hard, gym-muscled body. She'd got the impression he'd be fit—no signs of a middle aged spread on him—and she hoped her own body would live up to expectations.

"Bedroom, this way," she managed to gasp between bruising kisses. She remembered the condoms in the bathroom. "Hang on, I need to get something," she said, batting his hands away.

"No, Olivia, I want you now."

"I'll be ten seconds." She made a dash for the bathroom and found the condoms. Her gaze caught on her medication. Had she remembered to take that day's dose? She couldn't remember, but it didn't matter now. She grabbed one of the condoms from the packet and ran back to her bedroom. Michael sat on the bed, leaning back on his elbows, waiting for her. A slow smile spread across his face as she lifted the foil packet to show him, unable to hide the blush of embarrassment creeping across her cheeks.

He reached for her, took her hand, and tugged her onto the bed with him. He pulled her summer dress from her body, leaving her in only her underwear, and those items didn't remain on for long. She rid him of his trousers and Jockey shorts, too, so they were naked.

They fell together, kissing with renewed urgency, his hands in her hair, her running her fingers down the hard muscles of his back. His hand slipped between her thighs, his fingers curling inside her, making her cry out, making her wet for him. She rolled the condom down his length, and he thrust inside her, deep and hard, sinking down right to the base of him. They clutched each other as he moved, grunting.

Her eyes squeezed shut, but he reached up and held her jaw, forcing her to face him as he hovered above her, his expression almost angry. "Look at me, Olivia. I want to look into your eyes when you come."

His hips slammed against hers, as he looked down into her face. There was something dangerous in his eyes, but sexy, and as her world exploded in a million sparks and her mind was set spinning with pleasure, she wondered just how dangerous he would end up being.

Chapter Nine
Present Day

SHE ROLLED HER SHOULDERS to loosen her muscles and stared at her handiwork. A criss-cross of stripes ran across his skin, blood running down the cuts in places. Not all of them had bled, but all had hurt. She'd seen it in the way his body tensed at every strike, how he'd tried to pull away, even though his movements were limited as he hung from the metal hook in the ceiling.

She wondered what the hook had been used for originally. Whoever had installed it probably hadn't had this in mind. It was more likely supposed to be used to hang meat—pheasants or rabbits that needed to be hung for a while before eating, perhaps.

She risked circling around him to see his face. He wasn't unconscious this time, despite the whipping she'd given him. His shoulders heaved as he sucked in air through his nose, and the muscles in his shoulders and arms trembled from the exertion of holding his bodyweight. Something in her chest tightened, but she pushed the feeling away. She couldn't allow herself to feel any pity for him. Weakness was exactly what he preyed upon, and she needed to be strong. This wasn't for her; she needed to remember that.

She came to a halt in front of him. "Are you ready to tell me yet?"

He lifted his face to hers. Sweat beaded his brow and upper lip, and a trail of diluted blood ran from his hairline and down his face. He glared at her, his eyes still filled with tumultuous fury. Even if he motioned that he'd given in and would tell her what she needed to know, she couldn't be sure he would do it.

She found herself staring too long, locked into his gaze, as though he was seeing right into her. She dragged her line of sight away, not trusting herself to look at him for too long.

Could he control her via eye contact alone? She doubted it, but she couldn't take any risks. She didn't trust herself around him, and there was good reason for that. Right now he looked defenceless, strung up like an animal, but he was the one who'd caused all of this. They wouldn't be in this position if it wasn't for him.

"Don't make me keep doing this," she said, hating the pleading tone that entered her voice. "Just tell me."

A muscle twitched in his jaw, and he blinked, once, twice. Was he trying to tell her something? But then she realised sweat was running into his eyes, stinging them. Automatically, she stepped forward again, planning to wipe the sweat from his face with the sleeve of her shirt, but she stopped herself. She hated how her instinct was still to make him comfortable. He didn't deserve her sympathy.

Time was running out.

"I swear to God, you think this is painful, but what I've done is nothing. Don't test my patience. I can do worse ... Far worse."

She didn't want to have to, though. The idea turned her stomach. She wasn't a bad person. She had to keep reminding herself of that. She was only doing what was necessary.

He tried to speak against the gag, a muffled growl. Still frightened of him, she stepped back and jammed both hands against her ears. Though she knew she wouldn't be able to understand what he was saying, a fear lay deep within her. Feeling like a child, but unable to stop herself, she chanted to drown out his voice. It was nonsense, but at least she couldn't hear him.

She risked a peep over to him. His brow had creased in confusion, a combination of uncertainty and fear in his eyes. It looked as though he'd stopped trying to speak, however, so she took her hands off her ears.

Above their heads, a door slammed.

Fuck.

Someone else was here.

Her heart hammered, and she froze, her ears straining. She thought she'd prepared for this. No one else was supposed to be here now.

She trained her gaze across the ceiling as footsteps landed, one after the other. They crossed the floor, then paused and turned in the other direction. She looked to the staircase leading to the next floor and the door at the top. She'd bolted the lock, but if someone tried the door, they'd wonder why they couldn't get access.

All her attention had been on the movement of the person above, but she suddenly remembered the man. He'd also frozen, staring up at the ceiling, and she watched the change in his expression as what the movement meant sank in.

"No!" she hissed. "Don't you dare!"

But he did, inhaling deep through his nose, causing his chest to expand, and then he yelled best he could against the gag. The noise was still muffled, but to her it sounded painfully loud. She couldn't allow him to continue like that. If the person came to the locked door, they'd be sure to hear him. They might have even heard him already. She couldn't risk another person coming in here, or calling the police. He would do what he'd always done, and get away with everything with no repercussions. They'd get caught up in processing and paperwork, and before they knew it, they would have run out of time, and then it would be too late. Maybe it was already too late. She had no way of knowing for sure until she was able to get him to speak, but if whoever was upstairs found them, this would all be over.

Panic launched her into overdrive. "No!" she hissed. "Shut up, shut up."

She wasn't thinking things through now, only working on instinct. Frantic, she glanced from side to side, taking in her surroundings, trying to figure out if there was anything down here she could use. Cardboard boxes were stacked along one wall, the sides sagging and threatening to spill the contents. Along another wall stood a large wooden wine rack, emptied of any wine, but still containing dust covered empty wine bottles that must have been used for self-brewing.

Not wasting any more time, she took the couple of steps towards the wine rack and snatched out one of the bottles. Her fingers left marks in the thick dust on the glass. He yelled through the gag again, and she tightened her fingers around the neck of the bottle and swung it, her lip curled, her eyes wide. She must have looked barbaric, and the small part of her brain that was still focused, almost watching her from the outside in, rippled in fear. But there was nothing more she could do. Her arm curved in an arc, the bottle clutched between her fingers. It connected with the side of his skull with a crack that sounded hideously loud at a time when she wanted to be quiet, but he immediately fell silent. His head dropped again, his chin hitting his chest, and she stood, frozen, gripping the bottle in her hand and breathing hard. Had whoever was upstairs heard that? She realised how lucky she'd been that the bottle hadn't broken. The glass breaking would have been louder than the yell.

She strained her ears, trying to pick up the footsteps above. There was nothing. Had the person gone still because they thought they'd heard something and were listening for more? Her blood thumped in her ears, too loud, drowning out all other sound. She tried to make her breathing shallower, making it easier to hear what was happening above. Would they come to the door? Would they check the handle and discover it locked, and that would raise their suspicions? Tears of fear filled her eyes. She didn't want to be forced into a situation where she'd have to make a decision about what to do about another person revealing what she was doing. She knew they'd never understand.

But as she stood, breath held and pulse racing, the footsteps crossed back over to where the front door was positioned. She jumped as the front door slammed shut, and then exhaled a sigh of relief. Whoever that had been was gone now.

She turned her attention to the man, and the realisation of what she'd done sank in. He was unconscious again, which meant he wouldn't be answering any of her questions until he woke.

She hoped, by then, it wouldn't be too late.

Chapter Ten
Three Weeks Earlier

MICHAEL STAYED AROUND for the rest of the weekend. They had sex again, several more times, and Olivia made a mental note that she would need to replace the condoms. The box was now looking decidedly emptier than it had before.

When Sunday morning rolled around, she didn't want him to leave. But Tammy would be back soon, and she wanted to avoid having to introduce them. They'd end up meeting eventually, but she'd rather not do it when Tammy was back from another binge-partying weekend and in a foul mood, which she was bound to be. Tamsin never liked the come-downs. Besides, Liv wanted to keep Michael all to herself for the moment. Her friends would overanalyse everything, and she didn't want anyone to try to bring her down from her own personal little high.

Her flatmate wouldn't be back until the evening, however, so Liv figured they might as well enjoy what was left of the weekend. They ordered pizza in and hung out on the couch. Liv's heart was full to bursting. After the positively mundane start to the Saturday, things had gone decidedly in her favour.

Within thirty minutes, the door buzzed, and Liv jumped out of Michael's arms. "I'll get it."

She hit the buzzer to let the delivery guy up then opened the door to wait. She'd already paid by card when she'd ordered, so she didn't need to worry about the cash. The lift door slid open, and a man stepped out. He was holding a basket in both hands, so she wasn't able to see his face initially, but as he turned towards the door, confusion rippled through her.

"Tony?"

It was bizarre seeing her boss here. She almost didn't recognise him out of context. He wasn't wearing one of the badly fitted suits he normally wore to the office, but instead was in dark blue jeans and a striped shirt. His hair looked different as well, as though he'd used even more product than normal, and as he stepped closer, she got a whiff of aftershave. Had he stopped by here on his way to a date?

"Olivia, hello." His cheeks had flared pink, but he took a step closer. His gaze darted around, not quite landing anywhere. "I hope it's all right me stopping by. I'd been worried about you being ill, and I just wanted to bring you this."

She cast her gaze to the basket he thrust towards her. Cellophane covered the top, a white ribbon tied to the handle. Beneath the cellophane were bunches of grapes, piles of shiny red apples, the dimpled skin of oranges, and the hairy coats of kiwi fruit.

Liv blinked in surprise. "What is all this?"

He pushed the basket into her hands and cleared his throat. "Like I said, I knew you were sick, and I thought you might appreciate these."

Guilt swept through her, but with it came awkwardness. "I don't know what to say. I mean, thanks, but I only picked up a bug. It wasn't as though I was in hospital or anything." She felt horrible that he'd gone to so much effort when she'd basically lied to him about being sick. It wasn't that she hadn't been ill, but not in the way she'd told him.

Movement came from behind her, and she glanced over her shoulder to see Michael standing in the doorway. He was bare-chested and stood with his elbow pressed against the door-frame in a casual stance that left nothing to the imagination. Without a doubt, he was letting the other man know he was the one who belonged here.

"Everything okay, Livvy?" Michael asked.

Her cheeks heated, now sandwiched between her boss and the guy she'd been screwing all weekend. "Err ... Yes, of course. Tony is my boss, and he was just dropping this off to me."

Michael's eyebrows lifted. "Did you win a raffle or something? Couldn't it have waited until tomorrow morning?"

Fear that Michael would mention something about them being out together the night before she'd called in sick caught her in its clutches. Sharp nails of panic clawed through her, and she desperately wanted these two men to be apart.

She threw a nervous smile at Michael, willing him with her eyes to back away. "Why don't you wait inside and listen out for the delivery guy? He might be trying my mobile phone if he can't find this address."

"Oh, right, sure." A frown marked his brow, but he did as she said and turned and went back into the flat.

She turned back to Tony. "This was really sweet of you, Tony, but I really do have to get back."

"Of course. You have company." He shook his head. "Stupid of me."

"No, not at all. Like I said, it was really thoughtful. Maybe I'll bring this into the office tomorrow to share around." She forced a smile. "They will make a change to all those biscuits and cakes we're normally stuffing ourselves with."

He was already backing away, and the fist that had clutched at her stomach since she'd first realised who was here released its grip.

"You'll be coming in tomorrow?" he asked, not meeting her eye.

"Absolutely. I'm all better now." She kept the smile glued to her face, but it felt like a mask.

"Good, good," he muttered, his head down, hunching into his shoulders. "See you tomorrow, then."

He didn't even look at her as he disappeared back inside the lift and the door slid shut behind him.

Liv exhaled a sigh of relief, and her whole body sagged. That had been weird. And awkward. And now it was going to be awkward when she went in to work tomorrow, too. She looked down at the fruit basket she had clutched to her chest. What the hell had he been thinking?

With another sigh, she turned and went back into the flat. Michael was sitting on the couch, his fist balled and his knuckles pressed to his lips as he held in a smirk.

She lifted her eyebrows at him in warning. "Don't you dare."

He snorted out the laughter he'd been holding back. "I'm sorry. But what the hell was that all about? A fruit basket?"

She set it down on the coffee table and covered her face with both hands. "I know! Oh, my God. That was so fucking weird."

"He's definitely got a thing for you."

"No, he hasn't! That was just his way of being nice. He doesn't have many friends or anything."

The smirk was back. "Yeah, wonder why?"

She picked up a cushion from the chair and lobbed it at him. "Stop it. He's not a bad guy. He's just socially awkward."

"What was that he said about you being sick?"

"Oh, it was nothing. I felt a bit hung-over after our date, so I pulled a sicky. I'm feeling super bad about it now, though."

Michael laughed, deep from his chest. "I bet you are."

She allowed herself to be pulled into his arms, pressing herself up against his naked chest. He reached across her to where she'd placed the fruit basket on the table and pulled off the cellophane. He plucked a shiny red apple out of the basket and took a massive bite, crunching in her ear.

"Hey, I said I was going to take those to work tomorrow," she protested, pretending to grab the apple back again.

He held it out of reach, forcing her to clamber over him. "They're not going to miss one apple."

The doorbell rang again.

"Let's hope it's the takeaway this time." He laughed.

"Yeah, I hope so."

Liv didn't like surprises.

Chapter Eleven
Three Weeks Earlier

SHE WENT TO WORK ON Monday to a desk piled with paperwork she'd missed after having the end of the previous week off, and an email inbox she thought she'd never get to the bottom of. Though she'd told Tony she had her laptop at home, she hadn't actually got around to opening it and catching up on any work.

In the end, she'd decided to leave the fruit basket at home. She hadn't wanted to bring it in, knowing it would only cause everyone in the office to ask questions about where it had come from. She still felt awkward about Tony showing up at her place last night, especially as Michael had been there. Their takeaway had arrived not long after Tony had left, and they'd eaten, and then Michael had made his excuses and left. Though she'd enjoyed spending the weekend with him, she'd found herself relieved that he was going, so she could have some time alone to process what had happened.

She was thankful she hadn't seen Tony that morning either. He must be shut inside his office or out meeting a client. Either way, it meant she'd avoided that awkward moment when they came face to face, both of them knowing the real reason he'd come to her flat last night. She didn't know what she'd ever done to make him think she might be interested. He was at least ten years older than she was—probably closer to fifteen—and perhaps she was nicer to him than most of the other women in the office because she was grateful he'd given her the job opportunity, but she didn't think she'd done anything else to encourage him. She wanted to convince herself that he had come over purely because he was concerned, but it didn't sit true in her heart. She hoped that would be the end of it. Seeing Michael there would surely have been enough of a hint to let him know she wasn't interested.

Across the other side of the office, she caught Ellen's eye. Ellen's head immediately went down, hiding behind a curtain of her blonde hair, but not quickly enough for Liv not to notice how pale she looked, with dark smudges hollowing her eyes. Had her friend only just come in? Stupidly, the thought she'd given Ellen her bug went through her mind, but then she had to remind herself that she'd not actually been sick, had she? Perhaps she had, and that was why she'd felt so awful. She'd put it down to a hangover, but she might have picked up something, but it hadn't come into full force until later that night, after she'd already had a couple of drinks.

But Ellen's eyes were red-rimmed and bloodshot. She looked more like she'd been crying than anything else.

Liv slid out from behind her desk and went over to her friend. Ellen had taken a seat at her own computer but had the fingers of one hand pressed against her temple as though she was trying to hide her face.

"Hey, are you okay?" Liv asked in concern. "You don't look so great."

Ellen sniffed. "Thanks."

"You know what I mean. What's wrong?"

She plucked a tissue out from a box on her desk and rubbed it angrily across her nose. "Ryan and I had a massive fight. He says he doesn't know if he wants to be with me anymore."

"What!" She dropped to a crouch beside her friend and rubbed her back. "I'm sure he doesn't mean it. People often say things like that in a middle of an argument. He probably just said it to hurt you."

"Well, he did hurt me, and it wasn't even said in an argument, though that came later. He was acting strange on Friday night, kind of distant and sniping at everything I said and did, and then when I woke up on Saturday morning, he was just sitting on the sofa, with his head down, and his elbows on his knees, and then blurted that he didn't know if he wanted us to be together. He said he cared about me, but he wasn't in love with me anymore." Fresh tears fell down her face, her voice growing thick with emotion.

"Oh, Ellen. I'm so sorry. Why didn't you call me?"

She looked up. "I did. Lots of times. You never answered."

Guilt twanged her nerve endings. She'd been with Michael most of the weekend and hadn't even thought to check her phone. But then she realised she'd set the alarm on her mobile phone last night in order to get up for work that morning, and she was sure she'd have noticed if there had been a whole heap of notifications of missed calls from Ellen.

"That's weird. Hang on."

She went back to her desk to retrieve her phone from her bag. There were definitely no notifications, but when she checked the call log, she could see all the missed calls from her friend.

"I'm so sorry, hon. There must be something wrong with my phone. It didn't show me that you'd called."

"You didn't hear it ringing?"

"No, but I tend to keep it on silent anyway at the weekends. It's bad enough having it ringing all week with work stuff."

Ellen sniffed and nodded.

Liv rubbed her back again. "Try not to worry about Ryan. He loves you. I'm sure it's just a blip. Maybe he's frightened about how serious the two of you have become. Give him some space, and I'm sure he'll realise he's madly in love with you and can't live without you."

She blinked back tears. "I hope you're right. I don't know if I can live without him."

"Hey, of course you can. Don't say that! He's just a man. There are plenty of others out there."

"But I want that one."

She started to cry again and Liv gave her a hug. She didn't like to abandon her friend when she was so upset, but she was aware of the mounting work still building on her desk.

"I'd better get back to work. You going to be okay?"

"Yeah, thanks, Livvy."

"Any time."

Liv slid back to her desk and got to work trawling through the mountain of paperwork and emails. The time slipped by slowly, and she glanced up every now and then to check that Ellen was okay. Others in the office had noticed Ellen was upset, too, and made her cups of tea and dropped the occasional chocolate bar from the vending machine onto her desk.

A text message came through, and a call from a client, which she allowed to go through to answer phone. She checked the screen and saw the missed call notification come up. How strange nothing had shown up from Ellen that weekend. She felt bad that she'd been loved up and enjoying herself while her friend had been having her heart broken.

The morning finally reached lunchtime, and she and Ellen grabbed a sandwich together from a local deli, then sat outside, both nursing coffees and bottles of water.

"You didn't tell me how your weekend went?" Ellen asked between nibbles of her sandwich. "Sorry, I was so caught up in my dramas. Were you feeling any better?"

Liv suppressed a smile, feeling bad for her happiness. "Yes, it was fine."

"Just fine? You didn't do anything exciting? What about the new guy?"

"Well, I might have bumped into him."

"You did? That's great! How were things?"

The smile broke out across her face, and her cheeks heated at the memories of the weekend. "He came back to mine."

Ellen nudged an elbow into her side. "Oh, you dirty minx. You did it, didn't you?"

"Maybe. Once, or twice, or possibly three times."

Ellen gave a wan smile. "Lucky you. So when do I get to meet him properly?"

"Oh, I'm not sure we're quite at the meeting friends part yet. It's only been a week. It's not like we're serious."

Her phone buzzed, and she picked it up. A text message from Michael. She opened the text and read it.

Missing you. X.

"That's from him, isn't it?" Ellen snatched at the phone.

Liv held the phone out of her reach then turned the screen to show her.

"Missing you?" Ellen lifted her eyebrows. "And you said you weren't serious? That looks like it's getting serious to me. So, when are you going to see him again?"

"This week. He said he'd call me. He has a lot on at work, and I'm busy, too, what with missing the end of last week. I shouldn't even be sitting here talking to you. I'd planned to have lunch at my desk."

"You've got to take a break. It's literally the law."

"I know. I just feel guilty."

Ellen shrugged. "Don't be. You couldn't help being sick."

Guilt swirled around her gut. She almost told Ellen the truth of what had happened, how she'd gone out with Michael and had got so drunk she'd blacked out, and then hadn't been able to face work the next day. The words balanced on the tip of her tongue, on the verge of flying off. She also wanted to tell Ellen about Tony and the fruit basket, but she didn't want to make things even weirder in the office. If Ellen knew, she'd be forever teasing Liv about it, and anytime Tony called her in to speak with her or came to her desk, Ellen would be pulling faces or miming things at her, trying to make her laugh.

It was easier to keep her mouth shut.

SHE FINISHED HER WORKDAY and left Ellen with promises of keeping her phone close by so she could call if she needed. Ellen hoped Ryan would be home after work, and that they'd be able to talk things through and figure out what was going on.

It was a beautiful spring evening, and Liv couldn't bring herself to cram onto the Tube with thousands of other tourists. She also wasn't in a rush to get home, knowing that when she did, her flatmate Tammy would also be there. Tammy was never in a good mood on a Monday. Liv had heard her come in late last night, which meant she'd spent most of Sunday partying, too, so she'd be in an even worse mood than normal today. The idea of going home only to tiptoe around Tammy on a comedown didn't appeal.

Instead, she decided to walk and enjoy the sunshine. People sat outside at bars, drinking and laughing, while tourists stood taking selfies, and businesspeople marched along, swearing at the tourists getting in their way.

Liv wasn't in any rush.

She kept checking her phone, making sure she hadn't missed any calls from Ellen. She hoped her friend was all right, and had made things up with Ryan. Ellen and Ryan had been together for as long as Liv had known them, and while Liv thought Ryan was a fairly ordinary, basic guy, Ellen loved him. She didn't want to admit it to herself, but she was also checking in case Michael called, too. He'd already warned her that he was busy this week, but that didn't stop her heart from hoping he'd find time to meet. She hadn't connected with a man like him in some time, and though the prospect both terrified and elated her, she also started to think maybe it was time. She'd need to allow a man into her life at some point, and hope he'd accept her, warts and all. It was either that or she'd end up as a dried up old spinster with far too many cats, and she didn't even particularly like cats.

To her surprise, she found herself near Hyde Park Corner. She hadn't intended to come this way, but she'd been lost in thought, and her feet must have had other plans. The stands and stalls that were here over the weekend were still here, and Liv found herself slowing. Was she looking for the blonde again, the one she'd seen Michael arguing with? She hadn't even realised it had been playing on her mind until she'd shown up here. But there was no sign of the other woman. She hesitated near the stall where she'd bumped into Michael on Saturday. Should she go and ask the people who worked there if a blonde woman helped them out at the weekends. She could only assume that was the situation, as the blonde wasn't working there now. Even if she asked, what would she say? She'd look crazy if they did produce the woman and she asked Liv what she wanted. What could she say? Did she remember short-changing a man on Saturday? Liv would look as though she was trying to pick a fight, and the chances of her remembering one man out of the thousands who must pass through here every day was remote.

You want to know if there was more to it than he told you, a little voice spoke inside her head. *You want to know if he was lying to you.*

Liv shook the voice out of her head. She was being paranoid and ridiculous. And even if there was more to it, she didn't have any hold over Michael. Maybe the blonde was an ex-girlfriend, but he just hadn't wanted to tell her. It wasn't as though she'd told him everything about her past yet—hell, she hadn't told him anything, and there was a lot she might *never* tell him, so she wasn't one to judge.

With her mind made up, Liv turned her back on the stalls and vowed to put the blonde out of her head.

Chapter Twelve
Three Weeks Earlier

"WHAT THE HELL WERE you playing at last night?"

Liv sat up in bed, her head foggy from sleep, wondering what was going on. Tammy stood over her bed, her face puce with anger, glaring down at her.

Her mind whirred, trying to put the pieces together of the last twenty-four hours and figure out what she'd done to make her flatmate so mad. She'd grabbed something to eat on her way home, and then had managed to sneak in without Tammy noticing she was home, and taken herself to bed. At no point had she done anything to upset Tamsin.

She sat up and pushed her hand through her mass of red curls to get it out of her face. "What are you talking about?"

Tammy's glares didn't subside. "You left the front door wide open."

Liv frowned in confusion and shook her head. "No, I didn't. It was locked when I went to sleep."

Her flatmate jammed her hands on her hips. "You went out again. I heard you."

"You're imagining things."

"And am I imagining the door being wide open when I got up this morning? Jesus, Olivia, it's not as though we live in the safest of neighbourhoods. We're two women alone. What if someone had come in and raped and murdered us both?"

Liv scrubbed her hand over her face. She felt just as tired as when she'd gone to bed. "No one raped and murdered us. We wouldn't be having this conversation if they had."

"That's hardly the point!" Tammy declared.

"It's exactly the point. No harm's been done, and I don't even think it was me. I went to bed, and it was fine. Maybe the latch is faulty or something."

"What? And the wind blew it right open?" It was impossible to miss the sarcasm in her tone. The door to their flat led out onto a hallway with no outside doors or windows.

"I don't know what happened. Maybe *you* left the door open. You can't say for sure it was me."

"There was no one else moving around the flat last night."

She almost said, *you don't know that, perhaps you heard whoever left the door open,* but managed to keep her mouth shut. It would only freak Tammy out more.

"Look," she said with a sigh, "we'll both have to be more careful in future, okay? Double check it when we come in and go out, to make sure it's properly locked. I can't say any more than that."

This seemed to placate her flatmate—for the moment, anyway. "Fine. I've got to go to work." And she turned and stormed from the room.

Liv resisted yelling, *make sure you shut the door on the way out.* Tamsin could be such a headache at times.

How strange for the door to be left open, though. She didn't think she'd done it, but maybe she hadn't shut it properly when she'd come in from work. She had been tired.

She reached down to the side of her bed for her phone. Ellen hadn't tried to call her, so she hoped that meant she'd made things up with Ryan. Michael hadn't called or texted either, but then she hadn't expected him to.

Olivia hauled herself out of bed and completed her usual routine of shower, dress, and breakfast, and was soon on the Tube with thousands of strangers, all squashed together to do the commute to work.

Ellen wasn't in yet, but Tony was. He'd been out of the office all of the previous day, and she couldn't help feeling like he was avoiding her. She didn't blame him. She'd have avoided him, too, if she'd had any choice about the matter, but she'd had to come to work.

She'd barely sat down at her desk and fired up her computer when movement came beside her. Her stomach lurched as she looked to find her boss standing there, hovering.

"Everything okay, Tony?" she asked tentatively.

"Ellen won't be in today," Tony told her, not quite meeting her eye, "so I'm going to need you to pick up on some of the work she's got lined up."

"Oh, of course. Sure. Is she sick?"

"Stomach bug. Most likely got the same thing you had."

Her cheeks heated. "Of course. Poor thing."

No mention was made of him coming to her flat, and she wasn't going to be the one to bring it up. Out of nowhere, a flash of Tammy shouting at her about leaving the front door open jumped into her head. There was no chance someone else might have got access to the keys and let themselves in while she was sleeping, was there? Someone who was around her stuff all day, and who had already shown up at her place unannounced.

No, she had no reason to think Tony would do something like that. He'd only ever been kind to her, even if the others in the office thought he was a bit creepy. She didn't think he was creepy, just a bit socially anxious, though she had to admit him showing up like that on Sunday evening had been weird.

Still, the squirming worm of anxiety was wriggling away at her guts now, and she was struggling to shake the feeling that something wasn't quite right.

Back at her desk, she fired off a text to Ellen.

You okay? Let me know if I can do anything. X.

No reply came back, so she started on her work, going through emails and working through the pile of paperwork. She was struggling to concentrate, however, her mind jumping back to the open door.

Liv ate lunch at her desk to try to catch up, only using ten minutes while she wolfed down a sandwich to scroll through the apps on her phone, checking out social media. As she scrolled, a post caught her eye. It had been shared by several people she knew as acquaintances.

Local missing woman, London area. Has anyone seen Holly Newie? Didn't return home on Monday night. Police are increasingly concerned for her safety. Please share.

Olivia stared at the post, her heart in her throat. Was it her? The same blonde she'd seen Michael arguing with last Saturday? It was hard to tell. After all, she'd only managed to catch a glimpse of the other woman. Plenty of women had their hair dyed that same ash blonde at the moment, and for all she knew, it might even be different from the photograph posted here. But if she could convince herself of that, then why did her stomach churn so sickeningly, and her mouth run dry? Her hand was shaking as she held the phone, and she blew up the picture, trying to get a better look. The girl smiled out at a million strangers, completely unaware of what her future held.

Just because she was missing didn't mean anything bad had happened to her, and it certainly didn't mean Michael had anything to do with it. He had said he'd bought something from her at one of the stalls, and she'd short-changed him. That was no reason to harm someone.

Unless he'd been lying.

With a fresh sense of urgency, she read through the post again and tried to see any mention of a job. There was none, so she took to Google, trying to find out more about the girl. It didn't take long to track her down. It seemed Holly Newie was a twenty-three year old post-graduate student. Maybe she did have a job working the stalls at the weekend as a way of paying for her degree, and so what Michael had said was the truth, or maybe this wasn't the same girl she'd seen Michael arguing with at all, and she was just being paranoid.

She hesitated with her phone, wondering if she should come right out with it and ask him. She could say it in a 'hey, this is weird' kind of way, and hope he would dismiss her worries outright. But what if he didn't? What if he took offence and thought she was accusing him of something, which she wasn't, was she?

"You okay?"

Callie's voice made her jump.

"Yeah, sorry, miles away," she said, quickly tucking away her phone.

"You've gone pale." She frowned suspiciously. "You're not going to get sick on us again?"

"No, nothing like that. I was just reading about a girl going missing in London, and thinking how frightening that must be. We have to be careful, don't we? It's easy to get complacent when you've lived here for ages, but it can be a dangerous city."

Callie was looking at her curiously, and again the thought of how their front door had been left open all night jumped into her head. Tammy had been mad about it. Considering a young woman was missing, she guessed her flatmate had a point for once.

"Well, I hope she shows up."

"Yeah, me, too," Liv agreed, wishing that more than anything. At least then she could let go of the annoying niggling feeling in her gut that was telling her something wasn't quite right.

Chapter Thirteen
Three Weeks Earlier

"OLIVIA, CAN I SEE YOU in my office?"

Liv looked up from the paperwork she'd been elbow deep in to find Tony standing beside her desk. His thinned dark hair had been swept back with some kind of product, but it only served to make it appear thinner and greasier, the bald spots shining through under the unforgiving office lights.

"Oh, sure, Tony. You mean now?"

"Yes, now." He turned and walked back to his office, leaving Liv with a sinking sensation in her gut. Ellen wasn't back in work for the second day, and she hadn't replied to any of Liv's calls or text messages either. It wasn't like her, and Liv was worried. Was that what Tony wanted to speak to her about? He knew Olivia was Ellen's closest friend in the office. If something had happened to her, she'd be the first to be told.

Callie was sitting across from her, and she caught the older woman's eye and pulled a face.

"What do you think that's about?" she hissed.

Callie shrugged, her lips twisting. "I have no idea. You being sick the other day, maybe?"

Nerves roiled in her stomach. "He seemed fine about that. He told me to take an extra day and everything."

"Do you think he has concerns about your drinking?"

She blinked in surprise. "My drinking? I hardly drink anything. A few drinks on a night out, that's all."

Callie pulled that same face again. "You have been drinking more lately, Liv. I know it's normal when you've met someone new to get a bit carried away—"

"I haven't got carried away." Her cheeks burned hot. Was that what everyone was saying about her? Did they all suspect that she hadn't really been sick after all, and had called in sick because of a hangover?

She pushed her chair back and got to her feet. "I'd better go and see what he wants."

Nausea burned acidic at the back of her throat. Was he about to fire her? She needed this job. It was all she had. All her friends were here. If she didn't have it to come into every day, she'd be at a total loss. Tony had taken a chance on her at the start, training her up when she had zero experience with anything. Sure, she had a CV now, should she need to find a new job, but people would start asking questions when she went into interviews, and there would be questions she wouldn't want to answer. Just the thought sent alternating rushes of hot and cold flooding through her, and the room spun as a sudden bout of vertigo hit. She reached out and clutched at the side of her desk until it passed, and then put her head down and walked to Tony's office. She lifted her hand and rapped her knuckles against the door before opening it and stepping inside.

Tony looked up from his computer screen as she entered, and she was relieved when he smiled at her.

"You wanted to see me?" she asked, trying to keep the tremor of nerves from her voice.

"That's right. Take a seat." He gestured to the chair on the opposite side of the desk to his own, and she crossed the room and slid into it.

"I wanted to talk to you about the Richmond property."

It was all she could do to stop herself exclaiming, *thank God*, out loud. "Oh, you did?" she said instead.

"Yes. The owners live in Dubai, and I guess they've decided the time has come to cash in their investment. They want us to start showing it in the next few weeks, and I need the listing ready. The house could potentially be a big commission, if we can manage to move it."

Relief made her legs weak. "Of course. I'll do whatever it takes."

"You can take the company car while we've got the place listed. The property is a bit out of the way, and the nearest Tube stop is a good twenty-minute walk. I don't want you having to do that every time we need to show the place."

"Great, thanks, Tony." She perked up at the idea of having a car for a few weeks. Having one long term in London wasn't practical, but it would be fun until the novelty wore off. The car had the estate agent's logo blazoned across both sides, so it wasn't as though she was driving anything exotic, but it would still make a change from catching the Tube everywhere.

"And, Olivia, don't let me down."

"I won't."

She got up to leave, feeling one hundred times lighter than she had when she'd walked into the office.

At least Tony wasn't annoyed with her. She wondered why Callie had said that about the drinking. Had the other woman heard that Liv was getting the Richmond property, and had had her nose put out of joint about it? Maybe it had been Callie's way of trying to take her down a peg or two, though she'd never been like that before.

It didn't matter. The main thing was that her job didn't look as though it was in any kind of danger, and Tony wasn't holding it against her about the other night at her flat.

Things were looking up.

SHE LEFT THE OFFICE early, planning to stop by the property on her way home to take some photographs. As expected, the traffic was a nightmare getting out of central London, but once she'd got through the worst of it, she was able to breathe. She hadn't realised how tense she'd been in the office. Ellen not being there meant she was missing the buffer she normally relied on to make communication with the rest of the office staff easier, and what Callie had said about her drinking had left her confused and on edge. Plus, she was still hyperaware of where Tony was at all times, a part of her worried he might try to ask her out, or even that he would bring up Sunday and make things even more awkward. It might be strange to some, but work had always been a bit of a sanctuary for her—a place where she knew her role and was comfortable in it—but over the last few days, that seemed to have slipped away.

Hopefully, things would go back to normal when Ellen came back to work, and Liv could pretend Tony had never shown up at her flat with a random fruit basket. Over time, it would all be forgotten. She was worried about Ellen, though, and quickly glanced down at her phone to see if she'd returned any of her calls yet. It wasn't like Ellen not to get back to her, and she hoped nothing bad had happened.

There was a Sat Nav built into the car—something that was a necessity in their line of work—so it didn't take her long to find the big Richmond property. She pulled up to the front of the driveway, where a set of gates blocked the house from the road. Checking the bundle of keys Tony had given her, she depressed the button in the middle of the fob, and the gates rumbled and slid open.

She drove through them then hit the button to close them again. The last thing they needed was someone unsavoury getting access to the place. If squatters managed to get in, they'd have a nightmare trying to get them out again, and it wasn't as though they'd be able to show prospective buyers around with a bunch of people camping out in the living room.

Liv climbed out of the car and slammed the door shut behind her. She stood for a moment, looking up at the house. The place was huge. Six bedrooms, three bathrooms, four reception rooms, and a south facing garden. The front door opened onto a wide entrance hall with black and white chequered tiling, like stepping on a giant chessboard.

It was going to take her a while to get through the listing for the property and make sure she had enough photographs. The place had been standing empty for some time as an investment property, so was unfurnished, and would need some airing out before they showed it to anyone. People who had over three million pounds to spend on a home tended to be a bit fussy about how it smelled when they came to view it. People joked about baking bread when someone came around to view a property, but an unpleasant smell could put a potential buyer off as quickly as anything.

Liv got to work, making notes on each of the rooms and taking photographs to use in the listings. It would sell easier if it were furnished, so people could see how their lives would look already in situ, and she made a mental note to speak with Tony and see if it was worth the investment getting one of the companies they used to come in and stage the place. They still had a couple of weeks before it would go on the market officially, and sometimes you had to spend money to make money. This place would make an incredible family home, if indeed a family purchased it. She hated to see these beautiful homes just sitting empty while they increased in value, only to be sold on to yet another investor. At the end of the day, they'd sell it to whoever offered the right amount of money, but it would be far better to have children running the huge hallways, and for the massive country kitchen to be filled with the scent of cooking and the sound of laughter for once. She knew buildings didn't have feelings, but a strange part of her wondered if the big old house might be lonely.

As she was finishing up, she spotted a door beneath the stairs. She pulled it open and reached into the darkened space beyond, feeling for a light switch. A momentary stab of panic jolted through her—images of things lunging out of the cellar and grabbing her hand in the dark flashing in her mind—but she located the switch and flicked it on, filling the space with light.

Still, she hesitated before poking her head through the doorway. A set of stairs led down into what appeared to be a converted wine cellar. She looked up to where a large hook was embedded into the ceiling, and a shiver wracked across her shoulders. Someone walking on her grave.

She didn't like the place, but it would be a good selling point. People with tons of money always thought they were wine connoisseurs.

Lifting the camera, she took a couple of snaps of the cellar before backing up the stairs. She was happy to flick the light back off and pull the door shut behind her. It wasn't as though she'd be making the cellar the main focus of the house. There were plenty of other selling points, so just a mention would be enough.

Feeling she'd done enough for the moment, she locked the house back up and climbed in the car to drive the twenty minutes home. The traffic wasn't too bad, and by some miracle, she found somewhere to park on her street.

Just as she was climbing out, her phone buzzed. Her thoughts first jumped to Ellen, but then she picked up her phone to see it was a text message from Michael.

Need to see you. Miss you.

She stared at the message with a jolt of happiness, all her previous concerns forgotten.

She typed in a reply. *When?*

Tomorrow, after work.

Can't wait.

With a secret smile, she slipped the phone into her handbag. Everything else in her life felt like it was on shaky ground right now, but at least her love life seemed to be going well. She wasn't expecting it to last—these things never did for her—but she was enjoying what they had in the moment.

Liv let herself into her building and took the stairs. She had her head down as she reached her flat, so at first didn't notice the person waiting for her. She looked up with a jolt, her stomach lurching.

A blonde sat on the floor, her back against Liv's front door. Her head was buried in her knees, her arms wrapped around her shins. The first thought that jumped into Liv's head was the blonde she'd seen Michael arguing with, but a split second later she came to her senses and realised it was Ellen sitting there.

"Elles?" she said in surprise. "What are you doing?"

At the sound of her voice, her friend lifted her head.

Liv's heart crumpled at the sight. Her whole face was swollen from crying, her eyes bright red, her skin blotchy.

"Oh, my God. What did he do to you?" Anger replaced her initial sorrow. "Did that son of a bitch hurt you?"

She dropped to the floor beside her friend, wrapping her arm around her shoulders and pulling her in for a hug. Ellen shook her head against her chest. "No, nothing like that. He's leaving, though. It's over. I couldn't stand to be in the same house as him while he was packing, so I just came over here." She lifted her head. "You don't mind, do you?"

"No, of course not! You should have called me."

"I know. I wasn't thinking straight. I kept hoping he'd change his mind, but then he started packing boxes, and I knew I couldn't stay there watching him. Every time he put something in a box, I wanted to yank it back out again." She gave a small laugh, but it contained no humour. "Actually, that's what I did, and he was getting madder and madder. I had to get out of there."

Liv gave her friend another squeeze then got up and pulled Ellen to her feet. "Come on, let's get you inside. I'll put the kettle on, or maybe you need something a little stronger? I'm sure I've got a bottle of wine in the fridge."

She sniffed and nodded. "Tea would be good, thanks. I'm not sure I'd trust myself on wine. I'd probably only end up doing something silly."

A bolt of worry shot through her and she gave Ellen a concerned glance. "No, don't do anything silly. You call me before anything like that goes through your head, promise?"

Ellen nodded and wiped at her face with her hand. "Promise."

She let them both into the flat. She was relieved to see Tammy wasn't home yet. Her flatmate wasn't the most sympathetic of people, and there was still friction between them after the whole 'leaving the door open incident.'

Putting the kettle on to make the tea, she glanced over her shoulder to where Ellen perched on the edge of the sofa. "So, has he explained to you what's happened? Why he wants to break up?"

She shook her head miserably. "Not really. Just that he realises he doesn't love me anymore, and it isn't fair to keep living as a couple. He says he's going to keep paying the rent until the lease on our place is up."

Liv frowned. "He's going to keep paying the rent? How's he going to afford to do that if he's moving into somewhere else? Is he going home to his parents?"

Ellen shrugged. "I doubt it. He and his dad have never got on. It wouldn't surprise me if he's met someone else."

Her mouth dropped. "What? No, not Ryan. He wouldn't do that to you."

"If you'd asked me a week ago, I'd have said the same thing, but now everything's changed." Her shoulders shook, and she put her hands back over her face.

Liv quickly finished making the tea then brought the two cups over and set them on the coffee table. "Oh, honey. I don't know what to say. Do you want me to see if I can have a word with him? Find out what's going on."

"I don't think it will do any good," she replied between hiccupping sobs.

"Maybe not."

But Ellen hadn't actually said no, had she?

"You can always stay here for a bit, if you want. I know there isn't a whole heap of space, but if you can't stand to go home ..."

Ellen shook her head, and Liv tried to ignore the sense of relief spreading through her chest. It wasn't that she didn't want Ellen around, it was that she knew Tammy wouldn't be happy about having another person around making a mess.

"You're sweet to offer, but I'll be fine to go home once Ryan has got all his stuff out. I just couldn't bear to be there, watching him go, you know? It was all too painful."

"Of course. Whatever you want. But you're always welcome here, if you need to get away."

Ellen gave her a thankful smile. "What would I do without you?"

Chapter Fourteen
Present Day

"HEY!" SHE CALLED. "HEY! You need to wake up now. We don't have time for this."

Shit, shit, shit.

The blow to the head she'd given him to keep him quiet had been too hard. Now what was she supposed to do? She'd reacted out of panic, of fear that whoever had been walking around upstairs would find them. Would the person come back? Had they heard anything suspicious? She thought she'd managed to silence him in time, but she had no way of knowing if the person had left because they'd done what they'd come here to do, or if they'd heard something and had decided to either come back with help, or else go to the police.

The constant sense of the trickle of time passing refused to leave her. It chewed at the edges of her mind like rats on a sack of corn, leaving her frayed and anxious. She paced the floor and nibbled on her lower lip, her fists clenching and unclenching. How was she supposed to fix this? Would more cold water to the face wake him?

She came to a rest in front of him again. Every muscle in her body was taut with tension, and an irrational anger bubbled up inside her. Though it wasn't his fault he was unconscious, it still felt as though he was doing this purely to spite her. If he wasn't aware of what was going on around him, she couldn't even use the threat of more pain to get him to tell her what she needed to know.

Though it was of no use for the moment, she went to the small rucksack she'd brought with her. Crouching beside the bag, she undid the top and pulled out a notepad and ballpoint pen. It was the only way she could think of for him to tell her what she needed without allowing him to speak. She couldn't let him talk. That was where the danger lay. But if she could break him enough to prefer to tell the truth, rather than use the freed hand to try to escape, he could write down what she needed to know.

With a sigh, she let the two items drop from her fingers, back into the bag. She wasn't going to need them any time soon, not if he remained unconscious.

She had no choice but to try the water again. She had a second small bottle in her bag, but she hadn't wanted to waste it by throwing it on him. Aware that this might take some time, she'd brought water and snacks for herself. She hadn't wanted anything to drive her from this place until she'd got what she needed. There was a small toilet down here, so that wasn't a problem for her. As for him, he could piss himself for all she cared, and it probably wouldn't be long before he did exactly that.

With the second water bottle clutched in her hand, she got back to her feet. She cracked open the lid and exhaled another long sigh. She hadn't considered how much this was going to take out of her. Exhaustion weighted her limbs and made her eyes heavy and sore. All she wanted was for this to be over.

"Hey," she said again, raising her voice as much as she dared. "I don't want to waste my water on your stupid face."

There was no response. His breathing was shallow and ragged, his complexion pale, as though all the blood had sunk to his feet. His hands were still tied above his head, and she noted the tips of his fingers had turned a purple-blue, the nailbeds almost grey. Was his heart still pumping blood right around his body? At what point did gravity start to win?

She realised she'd just been standing there, staring, not acting, and shook herself from her thoughts. None of that mattered. She needed to focus.

"You're making me do this," she told him, even though he was unresponsive, and once more threw water in his face.

The water had the same effect as the previous time, jerking him into consciousness. His head rolled on his shoulders, and his eyelids flickered.

But then a strange noise came from deep inside his chest, and he started to retch.

She widened her eyes in horror, her understanding of what was happening sinking in. He was going to throw up, and right now he had a gag covering his mouth. If he was sick with that still blocking his airways, there was a good chance he'd either choke or he'd aspirate vomit, which would be just as deadly. She didn't want to remove the gag, but she couldn't have him dead, either. If he died, all hope would be lost.

With a cry of panic and fear, she dropped the bottle and ran behind him. The gag was tied at the back of his head, and her fingers shook as she worked the knot. His heaving body didn't help, his movements pulling the gag out of her grasp.

"For fuck's sake! Keep still!"

Finally, the knot came loose and she was able to yank the material away from his face. Just in time, as he retched a third time and his body was able to release what he'd been holding back. Watery vomit splattered the floor, splashing down his naked chest. She turned away, her wrist pressed to her nose, trying not to look. But she knew she couldn't just leave him. Without the gag, he was dangerous.

"Please ..." He groaned, his eyes fluttering. "Don't do this."

She couldn't risk him saying anything more. It looked as though he'd finished being sick. Working quickly, staying behind him to avoid the mess, she tied the gag back around his face, ensuring he wouldn't be able to say anything more. The hit to the head she'd given him must have concussed him, which had caused the vomiting. The reasons behind it didn't help anything, however. Now she had to deal with the result.

A few steps brought her back around the front of him again, though she was careful where she stood. The floor was covered, as was most of his chest and the front of his jeans. Having to throw up while your hands were still tied above your head obviously didn't leave much room for the vomit to go.

She spun away, her hand clamped over her mouth as she fought against the urge to be sick as well. She took shallow sips of air, trying not to breathe through her nose, nor inhale too deeply. Now what was she supposed to do? She couldn't stand to be down here with him like this. In the confined space, the air became permeated with the stink of vomit, and it wasn't as though there were any windows she could open. The only way to let in fresh air was via the door, and she was terrified the visitor would come back.

Her anger grew again, the same impotent fury that she'd experience when he'd passed out.

"Look what you've done!" she raged. "Look at this fucking mess! Did you do it on purpose? Did you think this would help you get away? That maybe I'd take pity on you and move you somewhere else?"

He lifted his eyes to hers and they rolled in their sockets, showing white forked with blood.

"No!" she yelled. "Don't you dare. Don't you fucking dare pass out again. I've been pretty patient up until now, but my patience is seriously running thin. If you want to make it out of here alive, stop fucking around and tell me what I need to know. Where is she? What did you do with her?"

But his eyes rolled again, and she knew she wasn't going to get an answer out of him yet. Perhaps he was just that little bit closer to being broken. The fight had gone out of his eyes, and she hoped it wasn't going to return.

She couldn't spend much more time down here like this, however. The stink of vomit was overwhelming, and she fought against her own gag reflex, not wanting to add to the mess. She hoped he was a little closer to telling her the truth, but she didn't think she could stand another minute down here, never mind an hour, or however long it was going to take.

She cast her gaze back to the stairs and the bolted door at the top. Did she dare try to sneak out and see if she could find a mop and bucket to clean up with? She'd be gone for less than a minute, and would come straight back in again. But it would mean she'd be leaving him alone. What if this was all a trick and he'd been hoping that by being sick she'd be forced to leave him unattended?

There was a second door in the room—the one that led to the small, windowless cloakroom. Perhaps there would be cleaning products in there. She didn't think she'd seen anything when she'd last been in there, but she hadn't been looking and so might have missed it. Feeling hopeful, she left the mess to go into the toilet. A string hanging from the ceiling worked the bare lightbulb, and she tugged it as she entered, flooding the small space with harsh illumination. She squinted—the light where she was holding him was far dimmer—but quickly her eyes adjusted. Was there anything here she could use? One half-used roll of toilet tissue was hooked on a metal holder attached to the wall, and beside the toilet, on the floor, was a bottle of bleach. Hopeful, she picked it up, but her insides sank again. The bottle was too light to contain anything substantial. Besides, she wouldn't be able to make much of a dent in the mess with only a few sheets of toilet roll. She needed a mop and a bucket.

Would there even be one upstairs? It wasn't as though this place was inhabited. But she didn't think she had much choice other than to go and look. Staying down here, suffocating in the stink of sick, wasn't even an option.

She left the toilet, tugging the string to turn off the light, and pulled the door shut behind her. She cast another glance over at the man. He was still conscious, but barely. With his hands tied to the hook in the ceiling, and how pale and weak he appeared, it didn't look like he'd be making a break to escape anytime soon. If she was going to do this, she'd be better doing it sooner rather than later, before he had the chance to recover.

Not letting herself have the time to talk herself out of it, she hurried for the stairs. Her heart pattered, her breath shallow, not only from her anxiety but also trying not to inhale. The smell was a little better at the top of the stairs, but only just. She paused at the top, listening hard. There was a chance someone had come back during all the commotion, and she didn't want to open the door and run straight into them.

As far as she could tell, all was quiet. With her heart in her throat, she pulled back the bolt. It opened with a crack, making her wince, but then she turned the handle and opened the door. Blessedly fresh air hit her, and she gulped it down, her eyes watering. But she didn't have the luxury of enjoying being out of the claustrophobic, stinking place. She needed to move fast.

Slipping out of the door, she went down the wide hallway, past the kitchen, to where the utility room was located. There was a sink and a tall cupboard in the corner. She went to the cupboard first, pulling it open to reveal what she needed, a mop and bucket. Then she checked the cupboard under the sink to reveal an array of cleaning products.

She sighed in relief. While cleaning up someone else's vomit was never her idea of fun, she was thankful for the products. She moved quickly, gathering up what she needed, resisting the urge to linger.

Being down there, with him, was necessary, but all she really wanted was for this whole thing to be over.

Chapter Fifteen
Three Weeks Earlier

ELLEN WAS AT WORK THE following day, looking puffy and tired, but managing to function. Liv was pleased to have her back, and fussing over her was a welcome distraction to being paranoid about where Tony was the whole time.

Liv was excited to be seeing Michael again that evening. He was taking her to dinner in a restaurant off Covent Garden. She didn't want to say anything to Ellen, hating that her new relationship was going so well when Ellen's had taken a nosedive. She was angry at Ryan for just ending things, without giving Ellen a proper explanation. After years of being together, Ellen was owed more than that. Each time she glanced up and caught sight of her friend's blotchy face and shadowed eyes, her anger towards Ryan built another notch. The two of them had been together for years, and it wasn't right for him to up and leave without offering to try to work things out. Ellen deserved better.

She'd met Ryan a number of times at barbeques and during nights out, or when he'd been dropping Ellen off somewhere. He'd always seemed like a reasonable kind of guy, and, as Ellen appeared more and more miserable as the day went on, an idea started to form in her mind. She still had the use of the agency car, and she'd be able to leave early again, saying she needed some extra photographs of the Richmond property, should anyone question her, which she doubted they would.

"Hey, are you going to be okay if I sneak off early?" She posed the question to Ellen, rather than Tony.

Ellen gave a weak smile and nodded. "Yes, of course. Hot date?"

Her cheeks heated. "Michael is taking me for dinner."

Ellen's smile grew a little wider. "That's great, Livvy. I'm really happy for you."

She hesitated, chewing her lower lip. "I feel bad abandoning you, though. I could always cancel, and we could do something instead."

Ellen shook her head, and Liv couldn't help but feel a little relieved. She really hadn't wanted to cancel plans with Michael. "Don't be silly. I'm crap company right now, anyway. You go, have some fun for me."

"Are you sure?"

She gave Liv's arm a playful shove. "Of course. Now, get out of here."

OLIVIA SAT ACROSS THE street in the company car, waiting for him to materialise. She knew from previous conversations that he normally finished around five thirty. Her heart pattered in her chest, her mouth running dry as she stared across to the office block on the other side of the road. She wasn't one for confrontation, but she couldn't stop herself from saying something. Her hands trembled in her lap, and she put them between her legs and squeezed her thighs shut to keep them still. Already, people were drifting out of the office block—some in twos and threes, others alone, normally with their heads down, looking at their phones. She tried to balance not being seen with being able to get a good view of everyone as they left. She didn't want him to spot her first and leave through a different exit. They'd met a number of times at parties or on night's out, so she knew he'd recognise her the moment he saw her, and he'd know exactly what she had planned.

He was one of the last to leave, and for a moment she was starting to think she'd missed him, but then she spotted him. Ryan was a little taller than she was, about five feet ten, with brown hair in a spiky cut, and a cheap suit. She'd never really understood what Ellen had seen in him, but they'd seemed happy, so she wasn't going to interfere. Now, however, Ellen wasn't happy, and Liv intended on finding out exactly what Ryan was playing at.

She swung open the car door and jumped out. "Ryan! Hey, Ryan!"

He glanced over at her, and she didn't miss the eye roll he gave as he realised who'd been calling his name. He lifted a hand in a wave and kept going. "I've got somewhere I need to be, Olivia."

She fell into pace beside him. "You've got five minutes to answer some questions."

He sighed. "I don't have to answer anything you ask me."

"Maybe not, but you owe Ellen. She's hurting right now, and she's not even sure what's happening between the two of you."

"Then Ellen and I should be having this conversation."

"Then why don't you? She said you moved out already, and you won't answer her calls and texts."

"I don't need to answer them. I know what she's going to say, and I can't say or do anything to make her feel better right now. She wants us to get back together, and I can't do that."

She reached out and grabbed him by the shoulder, pulling him to a halt. "And why not? Did you meet someone else? Have you moved in with her, and that's why you're still able to pay rent on your old place?"

His gaze darted away, and he shuffled his feet.

Rage boiled up inside her as she realised that was exactly what had happened. Ellen had been right. "For fuck's sake, Ryan. How could you do that to Ellen?"

"It wasn't intentional," he muttered. "It just happened."

"You're throwing away someone like Ellen for some fucking slut you've just met. You're an idiot." Her lip curled in disgust.

"I didn't just meet Sierra. We work together. We have for the last six months."

"Sierra?" she sneered. "Is that her name? What is she, like, eighteen?"

"She's twenty-one, actually."

She thought of something and looked around. "So, where is she now if you work together? Shouldn't you be leaving together now you're all snuggled up in a love nest?"

His gaze shifted away again, a muscle in his jaw twitching. "She had to leave early today. She had an appointment."

"An appointment? What kind of appointment?"

"That's none of your goddamned business."

The penny dropped. "A doctor's appointment? Is she pregnant? Is that why all of this happened so suddenly? You were seeing her behind Ellen's back, and then she comes along one day and tells you she's pregnant and that you have to make a choice, her or Ellen." Certainty settled within her. "God, Ryan. You fucking bastard. Ellen always used to say how you were one of the good guys, and all this time you were screwing some girl."

He didn't even try to deny it. "This is none of your business," he insisted.

"It is my business. I take care of my friends. I protect them. Don't you ever forget that."

His hazel gaze darted to her with sudden clarity. "What is this? Are you fucking threatening me?"

"Everything okay, Ryan?" One of the other men from his firm had seen what was going on and interrupted them. He was older than both of them—in his late forties, she guessed—and had the deep, stern voice of authority. She suddenly became aware that a number of people who'd also been leaving the office building had now come to a halt and were standing around, watching the spectacle. She bet they were just standing there, hoping for a fist fight so they could film it on their phones and post it to social media.

"Yeah, everything's fine. Olivia is just leaving. Right, Liv?"

She scowled at him, but her face flushed hot, while the rest of her body felt drenched with ice water. "This isn't over, Ryan. You can't treat my friend like that and expect to get away with it."

"Stay the hell away from me, and from Sierra, too. I mean it."

She stood, glaring at him, as he shook his head at her and kept going in the direction he'd been heading. Her whole body trembled, and she felt violent with her fury. She wanted to lash out at him, but knew she couldn't. Ellen wouldn't thank her for it.

Fuck. Ellen.

Was she going to have to tell Ellen that Ryan's new girlfriend was pregnant? Was it even her place to share that kind of information? She'd hate for something like that to come between their friendship. Ryan hadn't actually confirmed that her guess was right, so maybe she just needed to keep her suspicions to herself.

All the bystanders were drifting away now the entertainment was over, so she put her head down and crossed back over the road to her car. Her stomach had twisted into a knot that was making her nauseated. She should never have confronted Ryan. What had she been thinking? She should have learnt from the last time that trying to interfere in someone else's relationship never ended well.

She needed to get home and get changed before her date with Michael. She was upset and shaky, and a part of her wished she'd never come to speak to Ryan. Now she had information she didn't know what to do with. Ryan meeting someone else was one thing, but a baby? How was Ellen supposed to get over that? She'd be heartbroken. Liv knew it was something Ellen and Ryan had often discussed, even mentioning baby names, and which room they'd use as a nursery, should it ever happen. Now that dream had been stolen by someone else, and Ellen was going to be even more devastated than she already was.

Chapter Sixteen
Three Weeks Earlier

BY THE TIME LIV HAD driven home, showered and changed, and left the flat again, she was already running late. She'd texted Michael to let him know and apologise, but when she didn't hear anything back from him, anxiety buzzed at her nerve endings. What if he'd given up on her and left already, or was mad at her for being late?

She didn't like feeling so worried about everything. She was worried about how she'd tell Ellen the news about the pregnancy, plus she didn't want to upset Michael when things had been going so well. She was even still anxious about things going on at work—about Callie mentioning her drinking, and Tony turning up at her flat at the weekend. All the edges jarred her, leaving her unsettled and spiky.

She reached the restaurant flustered and certain he wouldn't be there, but she spotted him at the bar as soon as she walked in, and he lifted his hand to her to make sure he'd been seen. The hostess approached, but she waved the other woman away, pointing to Michael by way of explanation.

She hurried through the people, apologising when she accidentally barged shoulders with someone, eager to reach him.

When she did, Michael pulled her in for a kiss. "There you are. I was missing you."

The knot that had been winding itself tighter and tighter finally began to unravel. He wasn't angry with her for being so late. "I'm sorry. Work stuff came up. I couldn't get out of it." She didn't want to tell him about Ryan. It would look confrontational, and she didn't want him to get that impression of her.

"Hey, no problem. I know it happens. You saw that for yourself when I had to bail on you at lunch the other week."

She allowed herself to smile. "True. How did that situation end up?"

He frowned. "What situation?"

She raised her eyebrows. "The married work colleague and the secretary?"

"Oh, it's fine. All blown over now."

"That's good news."

The waitress arrived to take them to their table, and they wound their way through all the seated people until they arrived at the table Michael had reserved. She was still lightheaded and shaky from the conversation with Ryan, and she wasn't sure she was even hungry, but she could definitely use a drink.

"What do you fancy?" he asked her, after they'd perused the menu.

She knew better by this point than to order something that involved red or processed meat. She didn't mind anyway—her stomach probably wouldn't have been able to handle anything heavy.

"I'll have the crayfish ravioli and a dry white wine."

"No, starter?" he enquired.

She forced a smile, and then patted her flat stomach. "I think I'll save myself for dessert."

He returned the smile. "That sounds like an excellent plan. I think I'll join you."

The waitress came to take their order, and Michael ordered for both of them. Within minutes, they were brought a bottle of ice cold white wine to go with the pasta, and Liv didn't even care about tasting it. Michael poured her a glass, and she took several large gulps, both enjoying and needing the crisp, tart taste. She exhaled a sigh as the alcohol flooded through her veins, relaxing her.

Michael was watching with his eyebrows raised. "Tough day at work?"

She nodded, her face heating again as she realised how uncouth she'd been, drinking expensive wine like it was beer. "You could say that."

"Not your creepy boss again, is it? Do I need to go in and have a word?"

She laughed, half mortified, and half entertained at the idea of Michael going into the office to warn Tony off. "No, no. Not at all. He's been fine. It's a friend of mine at work—the one I was with the night we met. She's going through a rough breakup, and I kind of ended up dragged into it."

"I'm sorry to hear that."

She sighed. "Yeah, me, too. It's sad. They were a really sweet couple, but it looks like he's been cheating, so I'm not sure they're ever going to come back from that."

Michael pulled a face. "You know, I'd rather be talking about us than some other couple I don't know."

"Oh, right." She gave her head a slight shake. She probably had been going on about it, and it wasn't as though Michael even knew Ellen and Ryan. "Of course."

He leaned in towards her, his forearms folded across the table. "I had a really great weekend, Liv."

She smiled back. "So did I."

Their food arrived. Her appetite had returned, and the pasta was delicious. The conversation flowed as though they were old friends, and Liv found herself relaxing and forgetting about all the dramas.

By the end of the meal, she was loved-up and light-headed on wine. Michael insisted on paying, though she offered to split it, but he refused. "You get the next round of drinks."

"I can do that," she said with a laugh, putting her purse away.

"Shall we go for that drink?" he asked.

She'd been hoping he'd invite her back to his place. She knew he lived some way out of town, but it would have been interesting to see his home. She wasn't confident enough to say it, however, so she just shrugged. "Sure."

They left the restaurant and stepped out onto the street. He took her hand, and they walked side by side. A smile tugged at her cheeks. This felt so good—so normal—and she didn't want the evening to end.

"So, where do you want—"

A shout came from behind, cutting off her words.

"Sarah?"

The terrifyingly familiar voice sent her heart racing. Her cheeks flushed with heat, and she kept her head down refusing to look in the direction the voice had come from. Her grip on Michael's hand tightened and her breath grew shallow.

"Sarah!"

The call came again, this time more urgent, and hollow footsteps pounded the pavement behind her. She quickened her pace, hoping Michael would fall into step beside her, but he must have noticed her pull on his hand.

He looked down at her, his dark eyebrows pulled together. "Everything okay, Livvy?"

"Yeah, I just ... err ... I can't have that drink. I need to go home."

She dropped his hand, planning to spin off in the other direction. If the voice belonged to the person she thought it did, she didn't want Michael right beside her when the confrontation happened.

But she was too late.

"Sarah, would you wait the hell up?"

Her heart pounded so hard she felt dizzy, but she schooled her expression into one of confusion. Everything went into sharp contrast, the dark blobs on the pavement from years of chewing gum being spat out on the streets, the smell of heated rubbish on the air, the distant screech of a tube train pulling into a stop underground. She couldn't ignore him any longer. He was starting to cause a scene.

She turned to face the man she'd hoped she'd never have to see again. "I'm sorry. Are you talking to me?"

His blond hair was shorter than when she'd last seen him, and he looked as though he put on a little weight, but otherwise he looked exactly the same as he had seven years ago.

He squinted at her, his nose wrinkled. "What are you talking about, Sarah? Of course I am."

"I'm sorry. I think you've mistaken me for someone else."

He barked laughter. "Are you crazy? I know it's been a while, but you can't think I would forget you that easily."

She shook her head. "Honestly, I believe you think you know whoever this Sarah is, but she must be my doppelganger or something, because that isn't my name."

He stared at her. "Is this some kind of joke?"

"You're actually starting to frighten me now, and I will call the police if you don't leave me alone."

He laughed again, but it was a forced reaction out of confusion and uncertainty. "Call the police? I should be the one calling the police. And what did you do to your accent?"

She turned away. "I have to go."

He reached out and grabbed her arm, his fingers digging hard into her skin. "Don't you fucking dare, Sarah. Not after everything you did."

Michael stepped in. He must have seen something was wrong about this conversation. "What's going on?"

The last thing she wanted was to have him involved. "Nothing, Michael. This man's mistaken me for someone else, but he's going now."

The man from her past looked between them. Michael glared at him, challenging him to try something.

The other man pointed a finger. "You know her?"

Michael nodded. "Of course I do. She's my girlfriend."

"How long have you known her for?"

"Over five years now."

Michael's lie surprised her, and she tried not to let it show on her face. It made the other man falter. "Five years?"

"Yes, so you have the wrong person. I'm sorry." His arm slipped around her waist, as he guided her away. "I hope you find the person you're looking for."

She was trembling, something she couldn't help. The encounter had shaken her down to her core. She'd always thought of London as being the best place to lose herself, and had never thought she'd run into someone from her past. What was he doing here? Was he just visiting, or had he come down for work, or, God forbid, had he moved here now? She'd relied on the general consensus of people from up north thinking London was unfriendly and dangerous, and that they'd stay well away. The last thing she'd been expecting when getting up that morning had been for her past to come crashing right into her present.

Michael's arm around her waist tightened. "Are you okay?"

She nodded. "Yeah, he was just getting aggressive, you know? You hear of all sorts of things these days—people being stabbed in the street. He frightened me."

"Come on. Let's get you something to calm you down."

He steered her into a small bar. It was off the main street and was thankfully quiet. A coffee machine hissed. Music was playing, loud enough to be heard, but not so loud it would interrupt any conversations. A few other people sat around, all spaced conveniently apart from each other. Crazily, a memory from an old science lesson came back to her, about how atoms were like people on buses—they always take the furthest spot away from another person.

He ordered her a brandy and sat her down at a corner table. Every inch of her body wanted to run, but she knew doing so would look even more suspicious.

"Are you sure you didn't know him?" Michael asked as he set the drink on the table in front of her.

She picked it up and took a large gulp. The alcohol burned a trail of fire down her throat and settled to warm her stomach. She was grateful for the distraction, and the shaking started to abate. "I've never seen him before in my life."

"Really? He seemed so sure. He kept calling you Sarah."

She shrugged and focused on her glass, swirling the amber liquid around. "Yeah, it was weird." She forced herself to give a little laugh. "Maybe I have a twin out there somewhere."

Fresh panic surged through her. What if the man from her past started telling people he'd seen her? Would anyone come looking for her? She imagined seeing posters hung up all over the city, 'have you seen this woman' with her face plastered all over it. There might be a social media campaign. She'd have to move again. She couldn't handle that.

Or perhaps she was overreacting, and he'd go away and convince himself she'd just looked like Sarah. That he'd been wrong. He might forget all about it by the end of the day.

Fuck, she needed another drink.

Michael leaned forward and touched the back of her hand. "Well, you never talk about your family, Livvy. I've never met any of them."

"I've never met any of yours either," she shot back. "I didn't think we were quite at that point in our relationship yet." She didn't like where this was going.

"I know, but maybe we should start opening ourselves up a little. Meeting each other's friends, perhaps? I know you have some—you were out with a few of them the night I met you."

Unlike you, she thought. *You were alone.*

But friends she could do. Friends she could handle. And if it meant it took his attention away from what had just happened, then she'd hand him her friends on a platter, if she had to.

She smiled, though the expression felt strained. "Of course. I'd love you to meet my friends. And they're really curious about you, too."

He sat up taller and his eyebrows lifted expectantly. "You've told them about me?"

"Well, they saw me leaving with you on the night we met, so you weren't exactly a secret. Plus, they're all saying they never see me anymore."

He grinned, revealing straight, white teeth. "I can't have them thinking I'm monopolising you. We'll have to arrange an evening so I can meet everyone."

She was relieved they'd moved away from the topic of the man on the street who'd called her Sarah. "That would be lovely. They'd all love to meet you."

It was only later, as she lay in bed alone, that she realised he'd never mentioned his own family, or meeting any of his friends.

Chapter Seventeen
Two Weeks Earlier

BEING ACCOSTED IN THE street had left Olivia shaken.

The weekend was approaching, but she didn't want to spend any time out in central London, terrified she'd be spotted again. Instead, she went into work, and then came straight home, keeping her head down and praying no one called out that name again.

At least Ellen had been in brighter spirits at work. Liv hadn't told her about the pregnancy, and the longer she stayed quiet, the harder it was to bring herself to say something. She hoped Ryan would take the deed out of her hands. She hated to think of Ellen bumping into Ryan and the new woman, Sierra, and glancing down to see a large bump that had clearly been conceived when they'd been together. Ellen would rather hear it from her friend than find out like that, but still Liv couldn't bring herself to say anything.

It had been a long day, and, even though it was Friday evening, all she wanted to do was crash on the sofa with a microwave meal and a glass of wine. She picked up the remote control for the television and flicked through the channels, finally deciding on the evening's news.

Tammy was curled in the easy chair on the other side of the room, her laptop balanced on her thighs, scrolling through social media while she ate an entire packet of Wispa bite-sized. Liv didn't think either of them were exactly an advert for a balanced diet that evening. Her flatmate would be going out clubbing later, but none of the clubs even got started until midnight, so Tammy was just chilling out before starting yet another weekend of partying.

A headshot of a familiar face appeared on screen, and Liv almost knocked over her wine.

"Oh, my God."

Her tone got Tammy's attention. "What's the matter?"

She pointed at the television. "It's the girl. The one who—" Liv caught herself. She'd almost said, 'who Michael had been arguing with.' "The one who went missing," she said instead. "Looks like they found her body."

"Oh, how sad. Do they know what happened to her?"

Liv squinted slightly as she read the banner at the bottom of the screen. "Suspected suicide, by the looks of it. They found her body at the bottom of a cliff near Dover." Her pulse was racing, and she felt lightheaded and shaky.

"I bet they trace it back to social media bullying. Seems like all suicides these days lead back to that."

She wanted to say that Tammy was over-generalising, but she wasn't in the mood to get into a debate with her flatmate right now.

"Well, at least we know there isn't some psychopath wandering around London killing young women," Tammy added.

Liv barely heard her. Did Michael know the woman was dead?

Tammy looked at her curiously. "Are you all right? You've gone really pale, and your hand is shaking."

She put down her wine, which was in danger of slopping out of the sides of the glass, and shoved her hands into her lap to stop them trembling. "Yes, fine. Just always makes me think of my own mortality when someone young dies, you know?"

Tammy frowned at her in a way that suggested she didn't know at all, and then pulled her laptop back into place and looked down at it. The conversation was over in her flatmate's mind, but Liv couldn't get the thought of the poor girl out of her head. Should she mention it to Michael? Yes, she'd have to, even though it would be in a casual way. It wasn't as though she suspected Michael of anything untoward. Or did she? People came into contact with random strangers hundreds of times a day in the city. Not every one of them would be considered a suspect. Besides, the police said it was suicide, so the poor girl had done it to herself.

Even so, the urge to look Michael in the face while she told him about the young woman's death was too great to ignore. She knew it wasn't something she'd be able to shrug off unless she spoke to him about it.

She picked up her phone and fired off a quick text to Michael.

Are you free for a quick coffee tomorrow? Need to see you.

Her thumb hovered over the green key. She almost didn't send the message, nervous about what he might say, but then she bit down on her worries and sent it.

She clenched the phone in her white-knuckled hand, breathlessly awaiting a reply. What if he said he was busy, and then she'd be left to stew on this all weekend? She thought she might go crazy. The anxiety was back again, pecking at her nerve endings like the pigeons in Trafalgar Square. She took another couple of gulps of wine, hoping the alcohol would help to calm her. Callie was right—she had been drinking too much lately, though it wasn't for the reason Callie had assumed. She sneaked a glance over at Tammy, seeing if her flatmate had noticed anything was wrong, but the other woman was engrossed in whatever she was looking at on her laptop.

Liv's phone buzzed, making her heart lurch and her stomach tumble. It was him.

Love to. How about lunch? My treat. X

She allowed herself to exhale a sigh. It wasn't perfect, but tomorrow she'd be able to ask him about the blonde again, and watch his expression when he heard the other woman was dead. If he knew more about it than he was letting on, she was sure she'd pick it up from his body language.

Besides, she had no reason to think Michael was violent. It was only because something had felt a little off that day at Hyde Park that the woman's face had even stuck in her head. Michael had a few quirks, but didn't everyone? And he'd only ever been charming and attentive with her.

She was probably over thinking this whole thing.

THE NEXT DAY SHE MET Michael for lunch. She hadn't slept well the previous night, lying awake until the early hours and then waking up every hour until it was time to get up. The lack of sleep had done nothing for her mental state, and when she had managed to get to sleep, her dreams had been vivid and violent, with some faceless person chasing her in the dark. Her tiredness meant she was struggling to get her thoughts together, and no matter how much coffee she mainlined, she felt as though her mind was a tangle of worry and paranoia.

The place they'd chosen for lunch was a small sandwich bar that looked out onto the Thames. It was tucked away, but still Liv couldn't help worrying the man from the other day might see her. She felt eyes on her from every direction, and when the feeling got too strong, she whipped around, certain she'd find him standing there, only for the space to be empty.

She arrived before Michael, so she ordered them both a coffee and took a seat at a small round table in the corner. She didn't think she'd be able to eat anything. Her stomach was in knots.

Within minutes, his familiar tall, dark figure blocked out the doorway. The moment she saw him, some of her nerves eased. He was dressed casually in jeans and a light grey t-shirt. This was Michael. Handsome, respectable, caring Michael. She didn't have any reason to be nervous of him.

"Hi," he said, walking over. He leaned down and kissed her, and she did her best not to tense at his touch.

"Hi. I ordered you a coffee."

"Thanks. What about something to eat? Are you having anything?"

She shook her head. "No, I'm fine, but you go ahead and order something if you want it."

"Nah, I think I ate my own weight in bacon rolls for breakfast." He sat down opposite her and ducked his head as he looked at her. "Everything all right, Livvy? You seem kind of quiet."

She looked down at her coffee, twisting the cup in her hands. "Oh, it's nothing, really."

He reached across the table and covered the back of her hand with his much larger palm. "Yes, it is. If something is bothering you, you can tell me."

He looked into her eyes as he spoke, and she felt the sudden urge to blurt out everything. She didn't know why he always made her feel that way. All he needed to do was look at her and tell her to do something, and she found herself agreeing.

Her mouth ran dry at the prospect of speaking to him about this, but she knew she was going to. That had been the whole reason she'd asked to see him. The words sat on the tip of her tongue, ready to trip off at their own accord.

"Do you remember a couple of weeks ago when I bumped into you outside Hyde Park?"

"Yes?" There was still a smile on his face, but it was cautious now.

"You were arguing with a young woman, a blonde, who you said had short-changed you."

"Right?" he said, elongating the word.

She could tell he was trying to prompt her to get to where this was leading.

She picked up her phone and quickly scrolled through to the news article which had the woman's face on it. "Her name is Holly Newie. She was found dead yesterday."

He took the phone, the smile gone now, frowning down at the screen. Liv studied his expression, watching for any sign of an emotional reaction towards seeing the dead woman's face and hearing her name.

"Is this the same woman?

His comment threw her. "Umm, yes, I'm pretty sure it is. She went missing only a few days after I'd seen you, and I recognised her right away."

His lips twisted and he slowly shook his head. "I don't know. I don't think it's the same woman. I mean, there's a lot of blonde twenty-somethings in London."

Her mind blurred with confusion. "It is her. I'm sure of it." But was it? He'd already planted doubt in her mind. How well had she seen the girl, really? It had only been a glimpse, and from a distance. The woman had already walked off by the time she'd reached them. Maybe Michael was right, and she'd been worrying about this all completely unnecessarily. After all, Michael must have got a much better look at the woman than she had, and if he said it wasn't the same woman, then maybe it wasn't.

Liv gave a long sigh and reached across to take her phone back. "You're right, I'm sorry. I don't know why I was letting that bother me so much."

He smiled at her. "You care about people. That's a good thing."

She nodded and sipped her coffee. He wouldn't say that if he knew what she'd done in her past.

"Anyway," he continued, "when are you going to arrange for me to meet some of your friends?"

"Oh, soon." She was uncertain as to why a fresh set of nerves had started churning her stomach. "There's no rush, and Ellen's just come out of a long term relationship. I'm not sure she'd appreciate me rubbing you in her face."

He frowned and leaned forward, locking her with his dark gaze. "You promised you'd arrange something, Olivia. You shouldn't go back on your word."

"I'm not going back on it. I'll set something up, I promise."

"Next week, then," he insisted.

"Sure, next week."

She hoped his insistence didn't have anything to do with the man who'd accosted them in the street. Perhaps Michael thought her friends would know more about her than he did, and wanted to barrage them with questions.

It didn't matter if he did.

She'd always been good at keeping secrets.

Chapter Eighteen
Present Day

IT HAD TAKEN NUMEROUS fresh buckets of water, which she'd filled from the tap in the small cloakroom, emptying the dirty water down the toilet, before things had started smelling better again. She'd even taken some of the toilet roll and cleaned the sick off the man's chest, knowing she was probably going to have to get physically close to him again sometime soon.

He was fully awake now and watched her movements with careful intensity. The anger had dulled from his eyes, though, and she was pleased about that. Now she saw wariness, fear, trepidation, and that meant her plan was working. It was better that he was frightened of her rather than the other way around. His fear meant he was starting to understand the lengths she would go to, and that none of this was a joke.

With everything cleared away and the door locked behind her, she stood back in front of the man. She was exhausted, and from the way he hung, his head barely lifted, she thought he was, too. If only he'd just break, and then this would all be over.

"I need you to tell me where she is," she said.

He lifted his chin. Weariness haunted his eyes, dark coal smudges creating hollowed sockets.

"Tell me," she repeated, "and this can all end."

He sucked in a shaky breath through his nose. For a moment, she thought he was going to shake his head again, but then he nodded.

Elation rose inside her, wild and joyful. She resisted the urge to clap or punch the air. "Good," she said instead. "Good. Let's do this, then."

Turning her back on him, she went to her bag and took out the pen and notepad. "This is how it's going to work. I'm going to free one of your hands, and you write down her location. Once I've found her, I will tell the police where you are, and they will come here and arrest you. Understood?"

Something she couldn't quite read ghosted across his features, unsettling her.

"If you try anything, just remember that no one knows you're here. If you somehow hurt me, and you're tied up, you could end up dying down here, with no one the wiser."

This was dangerous. If she freed his hand to allow him to write, he'd be able to untie himself. No, she shouldn't untie his hand fully. She could just loosen it enough to allow him to bend his wrist and hold a pen. Then she'd be able to hold the notebook beneath the pen, which would let him write the location. Even his hand being loose made her nervous. But he looked weak and drained, dangling there. She knew he was a dangerous man, but right now she was the one who had the power. She needed to remember that.

Taking a steadying breath, she stepped forward, closing the gap between them. The bitter tang of his body odour hit her nostrils, but at least the stink of vomit had lessened. She wouldn't have been able to get this close to him if it hadn't. She was weak and shaky, but she needed to hide how she really felt. He'd sense the weakness in her and use it to his advantage. She was all too aware of his size compared to hers, and even with his hands tied, and with a concussion and after suffering a beating, he could still overpower her physically.

At the last minute, she remembered the cane. It wasn't much of a weapon, but it was all she had. She might need to use both hands to loosen the knot around his hands, but if she had the cane close, clamped under her arm or between her thighs, at least it would be on hand to use it if he tried something.

He watched her warily from the side of his eye as she approached, the cane clutched in one hand, the notepad and pen in the other. She just needed to be brave for a little longer. She'd already done the hard part. As soon as he wrote down the location, this would all be over.

Needing her hands free, and realising she wasn't able to put anything under her arm when she had to reach up high, she stopped at his side and shoved the items she was holding between her thighs. She stood on tiptoes to access the rope around his wrists. He continued to glare at her, but she did her best to ignore him.

Just a little longer, and this will all be over. You will have saved a life.

It was going to be a delicate balance—loosening the rope enough to let him move his hand, without it being so lose that he'd be able to yank himself free. Her fingertips found the knots, and she picked away at the one holding his right hand to the metal hook in the ceiling.

She didn't want it to come undone completely, terrified he'd swing his arm in a punch and send her flying, but it needed to be loose enough for him to have movement to bend his wrist and hold a pen.

The knot came free, and she allowed it to unravel the smallest amount, before yanking the ends tight again. The man struggled, pulling at his bonds, his body winding, serpentine, but she worked quickly and, as planned, hadn't given him enough to do anything with. She put her feet flat on the floor then bent to extract the pen and notepad from where they'd been clamped between her thighs.

Adrenaline rushed through her veins, her mouth running dry. Her tongue felt thick and fat against the roof of her mouth, and she hated that she was going to need to get so close to him to get this done. He was already tall, and with his hands pulled above his head, she had to stand on tiptoes in order to bring the notepad into a position where he'd be able to write on the paper it contained. Her breasts pressed against the side of his ribcage, but she leaned back as much as she could, trying to put distance between his head and her own.

She put the pen between his fingers. "Don't try anything stupid. Just write down where she is."

From her position, she wasn't able to see what he was writing, only the underneath of the notepad. But the pen scratched against the paper, the movements slow and deliberate, like a child newly started school, just learning to make lines and curves to create a snaky version of their name.

He stopped writing, though the pen was still gripped between his fingers.

With her heart pounding, she pulled down the notepad so she was able to read what he'd written. Finally, she'd find out what she needed to know.

Her gaze took in the words.

Crazy bitch. Fuck you.

Rage poured through her. "This wasn't the deal!" she yelled, glaring at him. "Write it down, you fucking bastard. Write down what you did with her!"

She pushed the notepad back again, no longer paying attention to her position in relation to his. She was no longer at the side of him, but in front. She was focused on getting the notepad underneath the pen again, and for him to write down what he'd promised.

With a muffled growl, he dropped the pen, and instead of trying to yank his hands free, he reached up, catching hold of the hook he'd been tied to. He hauled himself up, the muscles of his arms and shoulders bunching, and lifted his feet off the ground. It all happened too fast for her to realise his plan, but she reacted, bending to grab the cane from between her legs, intending to hit him with it again, and bring him back into line. But he used the hold on the massive hook to swing his body, and before she could straighten with the cane, his booted feet were in the air and swinging directly towards her face.

Chapter Nineteen
Two Weeks Earlier

OLIVIA SPENT THE WEEKEND hiding away in her flat.

After their coffee, Michael told her he had a lot of work on, and had made his excuses, though Liv couldn't help feeling like he was trying to avoid her after their strained conversation about the dead woman. She was relieved, in a way. She knew she couldn't hide forever, but every time she left the flat, she was sure someone was following her, watching her. Whenever she caught a glimpse of a man with blond hair, her stomach lurched into her throat, and she had to grind her feet to the floor, forcing herself not to turn and bolt in the other direction.

She didn't even want to spend time with Ellen, the secret she was hiding from her friend eating away at her. Every moment they spent together, it was all Liv could think about, the words shouting loud inside her head.

Ryan was cheating on you. His new girlfriend is pregnant.

Still, Ellen seemed to be coming to terms with her separation from Ryan, and, when Liv tentatively mentioned the prospect of a night out to meet Michael properly, Ellen jumped at the chance. Callie, overhearing the conversation, invited herself along, too.

The idea of going into central London made Liv nervous, so she managed to convince the others that a new bar in Shoreditch would be a better option. London was a big place, and she knew the chances of running into the man again were slim, but that did nothing to calm her nerves. If it wasn't for Michael's insistence on meeting her friends, she never would have considered a night out. She felt as though she was conducting a balancing act—trying to keep Michael happy while also trying to keep her head down. She hoped he wouldn't mention the 'Sarah' incident to Ellen or Callie. They'd be less likely to let things drop.

Her work week went by without incident. She'd arranged with everyone to go out on the Friday night after work, and had exchanged a few texts with Michael to let him know what the plans were. Still, she couldn't shake the feeling that he had been distant since she'd brought up the discovery of Holly Newie's body. Was he annoyed with her for doubting him? It wasn't as though she'd accused him of anything—she'd only brought up the woman's name. She told herself he wasn't angry with her, or else he wouldn't be interested in meeting her friends, and he'd been eager when she'd mentioned it.

She was probably just being paranoid.

LONDON HAD THAT 'END of the week' vibe, with everyone relieved to be out of the office environment and ready to enjoy the weekend.

Liv, Ellen, and Callie reached the place they'd arranged to meet Michael. Most people were still in their business attire—people in suits hustling each other at the bar, wanting to get served first. Liv scanned the busy space, trying to spot Michael. She didn't think he'd be here yet, as he had further to travel, but her heart fluttered with anticipation just in case.

There was no sign of him.

What if he didn't show? She'd be so embarrassed, making such a fuss to her friends about what a great guy he was and then for him to stand her up. No, she was overreacting. She'd known he wouldn't be here already.

"Oh, quick." Ellen grabbed her arm. "Looks like they're going."

She pointed over to a table where a number of people were rising from their seats. Other individuals standing were circling like sharks around a life raft, but Ellen threw herself into the middle of the throng, plopping her bag down in the middle of the table and loudly announcing, "Oh, good, you're going!" to the folks who'd barely had the chance to pick up their jackets from the chairs.

Liv ignored the glares of annoyance from everyone else, suppressing her smile at Ellen's antics. The people originally occupying the seats gathered their things and left, and Liv and her friends slid into their places.

"Right, what's everyone drinking?" Callie asked.

"Wine," both Liv and Ellen said simultaneously and laughed.

Callie disappeared into the crowd at the bar, nudging her way through all the shoulders to reach the front. Within a few minutes, she reappeared, holding a bottle of wine in a cooler, and three glasses clutched in her other hand.

Through the people, Liv spotted a familiar dark head, and her stomach fluttered. He'd made it.

She nudged Ellen. "Michael is here."

"Where?" Ellen peered through the crowds.

He spotted Liv, and she lifted her hand in a wave. "He's coming over."

Michael approached the table with a wide smile, exposing those perfect teeth. "Ladies," he said as a greeting, then leaned down and kissed Liv full on the mouth. She blushed with pleasure.

"Michael, this is Ellen and Callie."

"Hi, Ellen," he said, leaning in to take her hand and kiss her cheek. "It's lovely to finally meet you—properly, I mean. Waving at you across the dance floor doesn't really count."

"No, it doesn't."

He greeted Callie the same way and then looked around, his hands on his hips beneath his suit jacket. "What's everyone drinking?"

"Oh, we just got a bottle of wine. Do you want a glass?"

"Sure. I'll go and get one."

He vanished off to the bar.

Callie wiggled her eyebrows. "Very handsome."

Liv couldn't help grinning. "Yeah, he's not bad on the eye, is he?"

Michael reappeared with a second bottle of wine and another glass. "I didn't think one bottle would go far between four," he said, by way of explanation.

"Is anyone hungry?" Liv asked. "I thought we could order a couple of the antipasto boards so we could nibble while we drink."

He frowned. "That's a lot of cured meat, Olivia. I thought we'd talked about not eating so much cured meat. It's worse than smoking, remember?"

Her cheeks burned. "Oh, well, for the others. I'll just have the olives and bread."

"What's this?" Ellen enquired, leaning forward to hear the conversation.

She forced a smile. "Michael's been educating me on how bad cured meat is for us. Apparently a piece of bacon is as bad as smoking a cigarette."

"Oh, well," Ellen said brightly, "you've got to die of something. Might as well be something you enjoy, right?"

Liv tensed, praying Michael wasn't about to jump into a speech about living long and healthy lives. The last thing she wanted was for her best friend and her new boyfriend to start arguing. But Michael picked up his wine glass and lifted it in a salute. "It'll probably be the alcohol that gets me before anything else."

They all laughed, and something inside Liv unknotted. She didn't know why these two parts of her life meeting put her on edge so much. Maybe she was worried Michael would say something to Ellen about the man who'd stopped her in the street, the one who'd insisted she was a woman called Sarah. Michael hadn't mentioned it since, though Liv had found herself constantly paranoid she would see him again, and had taken to wearing a hat or a hoody when she was out, just in case. If Ellen knew what had happened, she wouldn't let it go so easily. Olivia also worried it would spark more curiosity into her background. A large percentage of people who lived in London came from other places and had moved here, but most of them either went home to visit or had friends and family come and stay. As far as all her friends and workmates knew, she had no one—a mother she had a rocky relationship with, and didn't like to either speak to or talk about, and a couple of fictional friends from university who'd since moved abroad. She was in her new life now and embraced it wholeheartedly. She'd put all the ugliness of that time behind her. The last thing she wanted was for her past to come tumbling in and ruin everything.

The group got along well, the wine flowing, and when the nibbles arrived, Liv deliberately ate some of the cured ham to show she wasn't having Michael tell her what to do. It was hard to tell how many glasses of wine she'd consumed, however, from the glasses being topped up whenever they were anything less than half full. At some point, a third bottle turned up, though she wasn't sure who had ordered it.

Feeling wobbly and with a full bladder, she got to her feet and made her excuses to go to the bathroom. Ellen got up with her and looped her arm through her friend's.

"We're girls," Ellen called over her shoulder. "We always go together."

"Well, what do you think?" Liv hissed at her as they made their way to the bathroom.

"He seems nice."

Her voice was too high pitched and she didn't meet Liv's eye. Together, they pushed into the bathroom. A couple of other women were doing their makeup at the mirror. The place smelled faintly of bleach.

"Nice?"

"Yeah. I mean, he's handsome and he's obviously successful, and he seems to really like you a lot ..."

Liv stopped in surprise. "You don't like him, do you?"

"I didn't say that!" she protested.

"You didn't need to. I could tell just by the tone of your voice."

Ellen turned to face Olivia. "Oh, sweetie. I don't know what it is. Maybe he's just not my kind of person. Or he's trying too hard or something."

"He's nervous. It's a big thing meeting you guys, and you all come across so close. It's hard for a man to fit into a group of women like this."

"Yeah, I know. But since when did you start not eating cured meat?"

"Michael says it's better for you. Is that okay? Is he allowed to recommend things to me, or should he have no effect on my life whatsoever?"

"You had a ham sandwich at lunch," she pointed out.

"So? It doesn't mean I have to follow his advice all the time. I can cut down, you know."

She flapped her hands. "Just ignore me. You're right. I'm still sore from the breakup with Ryan. I'm kind of anti-men at the moment. You could have walked in here with Ryan Reynolds and I wouldn't have approved."

"That's just because he's called Ryan."

"Yeah, probably." Ellen gave a laugh that didn't sound real.

"How are things going with the two of you?" Liv probed tentatively, hoping that Ryan would have been in touch with her and told her the truth of what was going on. At least then she wouldn't have needed to hide anything from Ellen.

"They're not." She sighed. "He still won't answer any of my calls or texts. It's weird. Since he moved out, it's like he's just vanished from the universe. He's blocked me on all social media, too. I definitely feel like he's hiding something."

Now would be the right time to mention her seeing him, and the younger model and the pregnancy, but she couldn't quite bring herself to say the words. It would upset Ellen, and though she knew how selfish she was being, she didn't want the evening ruined. Besides, it would be better to tell her something like that in private, not in the middle of a busy bar toilet.

"Oh, Elles, that's horrible. I'm so sorry."

"I'm sure he's moved in with a new girlfriend or something. How else would he be able to afford two rents, unless he's shacking up with someone else and isn't paying anything to her yet?"

"Well, we could always get somewhere together after my lease runs out on this place. Tammy can be a total headache at times."

Ellen's expression brightened. "Yeah? What about Mr Tall Dark and Handsome? You don't think you might end up heading down that route with him."

"Ellen, it's only been a few weeks!"

"True."

Was that even a possibility? The idea of growing that close to another person made her panicky. In fact, she wasn't sure she'd even be able to live with Ellen. The good thing about Tammy was that she had her own life and pretty much stayed out of Olivia's. Other than nagging about chores around the flat, Tammy didn't bother to get into Liv's affairs.

"Anyway," Ellen said, pointing to one of the stalls and hopping up and down, "I'm busting."

"Oh, sure."

Liv used one of the stalls as well, and tried to ignore the sickly feeling that had appeared in her stomach at the news that Ellen didn't like Michael. Hadn't she suspected this would happen? That was the whole reason she hadn't really wanted them to meet in the first place. Sure, Michael wasn't perfect, but who was? Certainly not her. She knew better than most how unperfect people could be, despite what they showed on the surface, and considering her history, she wasn't one to judge. But Ellen didn't know about any of that, and she obviously thought Liv deserved someone better.

But her friend didn't know her.

Liv didn't deserve anyone at all, not really, and especially not someone like Michael.

THE REST OF THE EVENING passed pleasantly enough, though Liv found herself conscious of what Ellen had said about not liking Michael. She watched their interactions with too much intensity, trying to figure out exactly what it was her friend didn't like. But by the time eleven p.m. rolled around, they were all tipsy on the wine and seemed to be getting on. Olivia's concerns melted away as she said goodbye to her friends and looped her arm through Michael's.

"Shall we get a taxi back to yours?" he asked as they walked up the street.

Liv kept her face pressed into his shoulder, partly to stay close to him, but also because she was still worried she'd be recognised. "What about your place? I haven't even seen it yet."

"Maybe another time. It'll cost us twice as much in taxi fares."

"Oh, sure." She tried not to feel the dip of disappointment inside her. "But we will go back to your place sometime, won't we? It feels strange that I don't even know where you live."

He laughed. "You know where I live. In Woodford."

"Yeah, I know the area, but I don't know what your house looks like."

He tugged her into his body and kissed her. "I'll invite you over for dinner, sometime, I promise."

"Deal," she said, though she noticed he hadn't actually given her a date.

A black cab with its light on was driving along the other side of the street. Michael lifted a hand to wave it down, and it did a U-turn and pulled alongside the curb behind them. They switched direction to reach the taxi, but as they approached the vehicle, a second man swooped in, pushing in front.

Michael pulled up short. "Hey, that's our taxi."

The guy was a typical London tough-guy, with a shaved head, tattoos, and sports branded clothing. He shrugged, his fingers still on the door handle. "Don't think so, mate. I was the one who flagged it down."

Michael's dark eyebrows pulled down as he glowered at the man. Liv stayed close, and she could feel the tension building in his shoulders. "No, I signalled it. That's why he pulled over." Michael looked to the taxi driver, who shook his head and lifted his hands, his way of saying, 'sort it out between you.'

"Just leave it." Liv tugged on Michael's arm. "We can get another one."

She didn't want for them to get into a fight. You never knew who was carrying knives these days. It was in the papers all the time, about how someone got stabbed over the most ridiculous of things—road rage, or because they'd looked at someone funny. Besides, she didn't want to be involved in anything that might cause her extra attention.

"No, it's fine, Livvy. This was our taxi, and this gentleman is going to let us take it, isn't that right?" He turned to the man, facing him, their bodies only inches apart. "You're going to let us take this taxi now, aren't you?" Michael repeated, staring straight into the other man's face.

The man faltered. "Oh, err, yeah. Fine. I'll get the next one."

Michael flashed him a bright smile of those white teeth. "Good man."

He moved past him and opened the back door, then nodded to Olivia to get in. The tough guy stepped back a little to let her pass, and watched as they both climbed into the back seat.

Michael leaned forward and told the driver where they needed to go then sat back again. The other man still stood on the street, watching them.

"That was amazing," Liv said. "How did you do that? I was sure he was going to start a fight."

"I have a way of getting what I want."

"Oh, yeah? Do you think you could get what you want from me?" She was flirting, and she knew it. But watching him stare down the other man had been kind of sexy, and she'd had a couple of glasses of wine that night.

"You'd better believe it." He gave her a wink.

Liv laughed. "I'd better be careful around you, then."

Chapter Twenty
Two Weeks Earlier

THEY TUMBLED INTO HER flat, laughing and kissing. Liv tugged Michael's jacket from his shoulders, dropping it to the floor as they stumbled over to the sofa. He sat down, pulling her with him. She swung her leg over his, so she straddled his thighs, their lips not parting for a moment.

Olivia was so involved in where Michael's hands were going, she barely noticed Tammy clearing her throat in the archway that led through to the open plan kitchen.

"Oh, sorry," she said, pulling away from Michael and widening her eyes at him. "I didn't know you'd still be up."

Tammy's lips thinned. "Well, I clearly am, aren't I? And I don't exactly want to be kept awake by the sound of you two shagging all night."

Liv took Michael's hand and pulled him to his feet. "That's okay. We can go to my room."

"I'll still be able to hear you." She scowled.

"Wear some headphones," she shot back, hating how Tammy was making her feel bad just for bringing someone back. Ignoring her flatmate, who remained standing in the same place, shooting them both daggers, Liv pulled Michael into her bedroom, where she shut the door on Tammy.

"I told you we should have gone back to your place," she said beneath her breath. "My flatmate can be a total nightmare."

Normally, Tammy would have taken herself out for the weekend by now, but it didn't look as though she was going anywhere. Maybe her plans got cancelled, and that was why she was still here. Liv hoped that didn't mean she'd be around all weekend.

He pulled her in, fitting her against his body. "We can be quiet," he whispered in her ear.

"Isn't it just easier to go back to your place? We can be as loud as we want, then." She knew she was pushing him a little, but she really wanted to see more into his life. He'd spent a weekend at her flat already, and it only seemed fair that she got to spend the weekend at his place as well. Besides, the thought of spending the entire weekend tiptoeing around Tammy if she stayed home was horrendous. "You did promise me dinner, remember?"

He sat on the edge of her bed and tugged her down to sit beside him.

"Livvy, I would love to cook you dinner, but the kitchen is a disaster. A pipe burst behind one of the walls and flooded the whole thing. The place is completely unusable."

This was the first he'd mentioned about it, but she didn't challenge him. "Oh, no. What a nightmare. How have you been cooking?"

"I haven't. It's been coffee shops and takeaways for the past few days."

"When will it be fixed?"

"Not for a good couple of weeks, at least. A plumber came straight out and fixed the pipe, but everything is saturated. I've got big machines in there roaring away to try to take all the moisture out of the floor and walls, but the whole lot is probably going to have to come up so I can get new floors laid."

She pulled a face. "I hope you have good insurance."

"Yes, thank God."

"You know you can hang out here as often as you want until it gets fixed. It's going to cost you a fortune in takeaway food if you can't use your kitchen for a couple of weeks."

He patted his rock-hard, flat stomach. "Won't be great for the waistline either."

"What's this?" Tammy's head popped around the door, and she hadn't even bothered to knock. "Sorry, but I couldn't help overhearing you inviting Michael to stay."

Liv rolled her eyes. She couldn't believe her flatmate had been listening in on their conversation. "Tammy, you're hardly ever here, which is fine by me, so you won't even notice Michael being around.

"This place isn't leased to three people."

"It won't be forever, Tammy. His house flooded."

Tammy scowled, her hands folded across her chest. "There's enough mess in this place without adding another person to it."

"He won't leave a mess," she said in exasperation. "He's not a child."

Michael lifted his hands and waved. "Hey, I am here. You don't need to talk over me. But look, I don't want to cause any problems."

"You're not," Liv snapped. "Tammy is the one causing problems, as usual."

Her eyebrows shot up her forehead. "As usual? What the hell is that supposed to mean?"

"That you have a damned stick up your arse most of the time."

Her mouth gaped open and shut. "How dare you!"

"Well, it's true. You party all weekend and then spend the first half of the week on a comedown."

"You're hardly averse to a glass of wine yourself, you know?"

"Yeah, a glass of wine. That's all."

"You were so drunk the other day, you left the flat door wide open. Don't make out to me you're little miss perfect, 'cause I know the truth about you better than anyone."

Her insides jolted at Tammy's words. "What?"

"I know you're on meds. It's no wonder you can't remember stuff when you're drinking alcohol on top of all that stuff."

She froze, horribly conscious of Michael beside her. She hadn't discussed any of that stuff with him, and had hoped to never have to. Maybe it wasn't good to keep something like that a secret from him, but she had far worse secrets to hide. She was frightened that opening that door would lead to others. She preferred for Michael to think she was perfect. Knowing about the medication was bound to cause him to start asking questions about her past and there were things she wanted to forget ever happened.

Tammy's gaze flicked to Michael, and a slow smile spread across her face. "Oh, whoops." She touched her fingertips to her lips. "Michael didn't know yet, did he? My bad."

"You bitch," Liv snarled.

Her head tilted to one side. "I've done you a favour. Now you won't have that awkward 'how can I tell him' moment."

Olivia leapt to her feet, but Michael's hand on her arm stopped her from launching herself at her flatmate. "Just leave it, Liv. It's not a big deal, I promise."

Tammy flashed them one last false smile then vanished from the doorway.

"It is a big deal. She shouldn't be telling you my personal business."

"I meant that it's not a big deal if you're on medication of some kind."

She sank back onto the bed beside him. "You don't know what kind of meds they are." Her stomach churned with nerves. This had never been part of the plan. She should have been more careful and hidden the tablets better from Tammy. It should have occurred to her that Tammy would have used them against her.

"Look at me, Livvy."

Feeling guilty, she turned to face him. He fixed his dark eyes on hers, his touch on her arm increasing in pressure.

"Tell me what the meds are for?"

His voice was firm, and she didn't feel she could disobey. What was it with him? It was as though he was able to just suggest something to her, and she felt compelled to obey.

The thought sent a ripple of unease through her. Was such a thing even possible? No, of course it wasn't. It was a ridiculous thing to even consider. Yet she found herself remembering the number of times he'd convinced her to go against what she'd really wanted. She'd thought at the time she'd agreed to please him, because they'd been a new couple and she'd wanted to make him happy, but was there more to it?

I won't tell him what the medication is for, she thought, turning her face away from him.

"Olivia." His tone was firm. "Tell me what you're taking medication for."

She lifted her eyes to his. She had to tell him. She didn't want to, wanted to lie and pretend they were for something else entirely, but she couldn't help herself.

"They're antipsychotics," she said in a whisper.

He frowned, his hand moving from her arm. "Antipsychotics? What are they used to treat?"

"I have anxiety. It got quite debilitating at one point, and I struggled to function. But I'm better now, as you can see. The medication keeps it under control."

"I see."

"Plenty of people have mental health issues at some point in their lives, Michael." Her cheeks burned. "It's not something to be ashamed of."

Lines marred his normally smooth brow. "So why didn't you tell me already?"

"Because I wasn't sure we were serious enough to be having those kinds of conversations. It's not as though you've told me every single detail of your health over the past however many years. In fact, you hardly tell me anything about yourself at all!"

"That's not true, Olivia. I've told you plenty."

"About work, maybe, about what food you like, and books you read, but I've never met any of your friends or family. I've never even seen your house."

He huffed out a breath of air in exasperation. "Like you pointed out, Olivia, we're still a new couple. There's no need to rush into all of this."

"You mean I have to tell you everything about me, but you can hold back everything about you."

"This is ridiculous." He got to his feet. "I need to get going."

Bitterness shot straight through her heart. "Of course, you do. Now that you've heard my dirty little secret, you're running straight for the door."

"I'm not running. I just have somewhere to be."

"Your flooded house, you mean?"

He jammed his hands on his hips and nodded. "Yes, actually. I need to meet a builder first thing to get a quote for the work to be done."

"So, let me come with you." She knew how desperate she sounded and hated herself for it.

His eyes narrowed. "You're being kind of clingy now, Liv."

"Of course, I am. Well, off you go, then. Wouldn't want a clingy woman hanging around." She went to the door and motioned for him to walk out.

He exhaled another sigh. "Fine. I'll call you."

Michael leaned down to kiss her cheek, but she ducked her face away at the last moment so he only got air.

"Right." He shook his head and turned and walked out the door.

Liv jumped to her feet and slammed it behind him. Then she sat back down on the bed, put her head in her hands, and burst into tears.

Chapter Twenty-one
One Week Earlier

SHE HADN'T HEARD FROM Michael since their argument. The weekend had passed with no contact, and then she started work again on Monday and did her best to put him out of her mind. She wrote and deleted numerous text messages, wanting to send them, but a mixture of pride and self-preservation held her back. She wasn't speaking to Tammy either, after what she'd done, and the two of them passed each other in the flat like the living and the dead.

Ellen had picked up on something being wrong, but Liv didn't want to tell her what had happened. Ellen had already said she didn't like Michael, and Liv didn't want to give her a good reason to like him even less. Deep down, she was hoping this was just a blip, and she knew bitching about Michael to her friend would only make things harder if they managed to come back from the argument.

Something else was holding her back from talking to Ellen, and that was the medication. If she told Ellen that she and Michael had fought, she would want to know the details, and then Liv would have to admit to her that she was on long term meds. It wasn't a conversation she wanted to have, so instead she stayed quiet and plastered a fake smile on her face whenever someone asked how she was.

She managed to get through most of the week. Work was busy, as usual, which helped to keep her mind off the lack of messages or phone calls she'd had from Michael, but she hadn't been sleeping well. She lay awake half of the night, worrying about Michael's reaction to the news of her being on medication. It was irrational, but she was also concerned that he'd start putting together the pieces, and wonder if perhaps she did have more in her past than she'd told him, and if the man who'd called her Sarah in the street actually did have the right person. She was terrified Michael would start digging into her past. But a first name wouldn't give him much to go on, and anyway, he'd most likely have just gone home and forgotten all about her. A man like Michael didn't need to lower his standards with someone like her. He'd probably moved on already.

By the time she got to Friday afternoon, she was exhausted and barely functioning.

"Hey, are you okay?" Tony asked as he caught sight of her hovering over the water dispenser.

She managed a nod. "Sure. Just tired. That bug I caught the other week must have taken it out of me more than I'd thought."

He frowned at her, concerned, and guilt coiled around her gut at her lie. No, it wasn't a lie. She had been ill.

"Knock off a couple of hours early if you want. It's Friday afternoon." He gave her a wink. "It's not like any of you guys are working up to your full potential anyway."

The wink looked strange on him, but she managed a small laugh. "As long as you're sure." She wasn't being productive, and

SOME THEY LIE 153

she was letting things fall through the cracks—forgetting to return phone calls she'd promised, and not sending an important email to a solicitor about completion on a property.

"Of course. Come back on Monday refreshed. And I do mean refreshed, Olivia. I'm not giving you time off to go to the pub."

"I won't, I promise."

She went back to her desk to get her stuff. Ellen caught sight of her. "You going home early?"

Liv felt bad she was the one skiving off, when Ellen had been through a far more traumatic breakup than the one she was currently torturing herself over. "Yeah, I'm not feeling great, so Tony said I could sneak home a few hours early."

"Hey, well, if you're feeling up to it tomorrow, do you want to get together? The weekends feel weird now Ryan's not around." She must have thought of something. "Oh, unless you're seeing Michael, of course."

"He's got something on this weekend," she lied. "He had a burst pipe in his kitchen and it flooded the place out, so he's spending all his time dealing with different contractors right now."

Ellen pulled a face. "What a nightmare."

"Yeah, it is." She forced a smile. "But it means I get to spend time with my best friend instead."

Ellen returned the smile. "Great. I'll look forward to it. You want to come over to mine after lunch?"

"Sure. I'll see you tomorrow."

Liv gathered up her belongings, and keeping her head down so she wasn't stopped and questioned by half the office, left the building. She still had use of the agency car while she was in charge of the Richmond property, so she didn't have to negotiate the Tube. She felt bad that she'd taken the car when she'd gone home early and wasn't exactly working, but it wasn't as though anyone else needed it. Most of the time, it was easier and quicker for the estate agents to catch the Tube, or even walk to the properties than it was to drive, so no one else would need to use the car, anyway.

Tammy had mentioned that she was going out straight after work, so Liv was relieved she'd have the flat to herself that weekend. Things had been unbearably strained over the past week, and she needed a little space from her flatmate. Though she knew lying to Michael was bad, it still hadn't been Tammy's place to say anything. She didn't doubt that if Michael was in the dark about the medication, then he'd also still be in her life.

As usual, she avoided the lift up to her floor and took the couple of flights of stairs instead. She was looking forward to getting home. All she wanted was a long hot bath and an early night.

As she rummaged around in her bag for her keys, muffled voices drew her attention. She looked up with a frown. It sounded as though someone was having an argument, and they were inside her flat, but no one was supposed to be home. The voices grew louder, and definitely heated, but then she realised the reason they'd got louder was because whoever they belonged to was walking towards the front door. Her heart caught as the front door of her flat started to open.

Instinctively, she stepped back into the doorway of the neighbour's flat, holding her breath, flattening herself against the surface. Her heart beat hard, every muscle tensed. No one was supposed to be in. From her view point, she was just able to make out a familiar tall, dark figure step out of her front door.

Her heart lurched.

Michael!

What the hell was he doing here, and, more to the point, who had let him in?

Tammy.

It must be. There was no other explanation. Either she'd let him in, or he'd cut himself a key. It made far more sense that Tammy had let him in, though she remembered how her front door had been left open the other week. Was it possible it had been neither her nor Tammy responsible, and actually someone else with a key? The idea sent fingers crawling up her spine.

Michael pulled the door shut behind him then crossed the hallway to the lift opposite. He hit the button to call the car, and when the door slid open, he stepped in and vanished from view.

Liv's mind whirred with confusion. Was he looking for her? If so, why hadn't he just called her? It wasn't as though he didn't have her number, and even if he'd lost it, he could have tracked her down at work. It didn't make sense. Unless there was something going on between him and Tammy, and they didn't know how to tell her. Was that why Tammy had been so against him spending more time there while his house was being repaired? Did she worry it would all come out about the two of them?

Her face flushed hot, and then a wave of cold swept over her. She didn't want to go in there, didn't want to have to confront her flatmate again. All she wanted to do was hide from everything or run away. No, she couldn't run away. Not again.

The front door opened, and Tammy slipped out, clutching her handbag. She caught the lift, too, the doors sliding shut behind her. Liv waited until she was sure Tammy had gone then took her keys and let herself into the flat. Her senses were on high alert, trying to spot something that could be used as proof that the two of them were up to no good. Her nostrils flared for the musky scent of sex on the air, but she couldn't detect anything. In a wild surge of adrenaline, she ran to Tammy's bedroom, throwing open the door. She checked the bed for rumpled bedclothes, placed her palms against the mattress to feel for the residue of body heat. Caught up in a frantic kind of madness, she searched Tammy's bathroom, checking the bin for a used condom. Then she remembered the packet in her bathroom. Still carried on her ride of adrenaline, she ran to her bathroom and checked the box. Were more missing? Yes, she was sure there were. Of course, it didn't mean Tammy had used them on Michael, but her mind kept going in that direction. Was that why she'd told him about the medication? She'd wanted him for herself and knew that would be enough to send him running. Tammy didn't know the half of it.

Finally, exhausted, she sat on the edge of the sofa with her head in her hands. Should she call Michael and demand to know what was going on? At least Tammy most likely wouldn't be home until Sunday, so Liv had some time to decide how to handle this.

What should she do? Confront them? Damn it. She needed a glass of wine.

She was thankful for the chilled bottle of sauvignon blanc in the fridge. Without stopping to think about how she'd barely eaten all day and hadn't slept all week, never mind whether or not she'd taken her meds, she cracked open the twist top and poured herself a large glass. She drank the first glass within a couple of gulps then poured a second and carried it over to the sofa. Her head was a mess. She knew she should pick up the phone and call either Michael or Tammy and demand to know what was going on, but she couldn't face it. She didn't feel as though either of them particularly liked her right now, and what if they both told her that they were together now, and there was nothing she could do about it? They'd be right, too—what *could* she do about it? She'd only been seeing Michael for a few weeks, and they hadn't talked about being exclusive. But even so, the idea of him and Tammy being together made her lightheaded and nauseated. In her head, she saw them kissing, his fingers laced in her silky blonde hair, and her climbing on top of him on the couch. She imagined them laughing together about stupid old Olivia, and how they had both never liked her anyway. No, she didn't want to think about it. How had this even happened? Her thoughts felt muddled and fuzzy, as though she was trying to piece them together when they were surrounded in cotton wool.

Desperate to get the images out of her head and to stop the thoughts from tumbling over and over, she grabbed the bottle of wine and poured herself another glass.

THE RINGING OF HER phone dragged her from sleep.

Liv blinked open her eyes and tried to put her thoughts together. What had happened? Her head felt groggy, her mouth dry. Of course, the wine. She'd drunk too much wine. But then she remembered the reason she'd drunk too much.

Tammy and Michael. She'd caught them sneaking out of here yesterday afternoon.

She reached out to grab her phone and answered without checking the screen.

"It's me," the voice on the end of the line said. Ellen. "Where are you? I thought we were going to the cinema."

"Oh, shit." Groggily, she checked the clock. With a start, she saw it was gone one in the afternoon. She'd arrived home a little after four the previous day. She'd lost almost an entire day. How long had she been drinking for? She thought she only had the one bottle of wine in the flat. Had she gone out and bought some more? If so, she couldn't remember a thing. "I'm sorry. I don't know what happened."

"What do you mean you don't know what happened? Are you okay?"

Out of nowhere, Liv burst into tears. "I don't know."

"Livvy you're frightening me right now. What's going on?"

"It's Michael ..." Her voice broke with fresh tears.

"What's he done? Did he hurt you?"

She shook her head against the phone, and winced as pain lashed through her skull. "No, nothing like that."

"Do you want me to come over?"

"No, no, I'll be okay."

"Bullshit. I'm coming over."

The phone went dead.

There was no point in trying to persuade Ellen from doing anything different. Once her friend set her mind on something, there was no changing it. She felt bad, as she should be the one who was there for Ellen after the breakup with Ryan, not the other way around. But truthfully, she was pleased her friend was coming over. She didn't feel right, lightheaded and shaky, and like she wasn't really connected to the world.

It's happening again ...

No, no, no. This was different. She had everything under control. It was having Michael in her life that was messing with her head. She should never have tried to get involved in a relationship. All the questions, the way she was constantly worried he would uncover something about her old life, had made her paranoid.

Though she knew having him in her life was too much for her to handle, the idea of letting him go sent pain through her heart.

He's probably already gone, she told herself. *It isn't even your decision to make.* He hadn't called or texted since he'd left last week. Why would someone like him want to continue a relationship with a woman he now knew was on medication? He'd be better with some nice, normal girl.

Because maybe he actually likes you, a little voice whispered in her head. No, he didn't. If he did, he would never have got involved with Tammy. Unless, of course, she'd read the whole situation completely wrong and there was a reasonable explanation.

Not wanting Ellen to see her in such a mess, knowing she must stink of alcohol, and that her feet were filthy, though she had no idea why, Liv quickly jumped in the shower, scrubbing away the worst of it. She brushed her teeth and rubbed some concealer beneath her eyes. She was worried for herself, but though she was going to talk to her friend, she didn't want Ellen to see her in all her stark horror.

The doorbell rang, and she went to let Ellen up. Ellen stood in the hall outside, her face pinched in concern. She reached out and stroked Liv's arm as she stepped into the flat.

"Hey, how are you doing?"

"I've been better," Liv admitted. *I've been worse, too,* she thought but didn't add.

"Shall I put the kettle on?" Ellen went straight for the kitchen and set about making them both tea. "So, start from the beginning. Tell me what happened."

Liv sucked in a breath. "You know I came home early on Friday?"

Ellen nodded.

"Well, I caught Michael and Tammy here together."

Ellen spun to face her, a teabag held in each hand, her eyes wide. "*Together*, together? In bed together?"

"Well, no, not exactly. But I caught him sneaking out of here. What other explanation could there be?"

Her friend bit her lower lip as she thought. "Maybe he was coming around to see you?"

"Why? He would have known I was at work."

"Hmm, true. Have you not spoken to him at all?"

"No. I didn't want to call him. I didn't know what to say."

"Okay, so is that why you were so upset when I called you?"

Liv nodded, and hesitated before she said, "Yeah, a part of it."

"What's the other part?"

She held herself back, unsure if she should admit what happened. But she was desperate to talk to someone, and she trusted Ellen. Ellen was the only person in this world she thought she actually *did* trust.

"After I saw him leave, and then Tammy followed him out, I went a bit mad. I drank too much ..."

"That's understandable, considering."

"Yeah, but there's something else." She took a deep breath to help her courage. "I'm losing time."

Ellen frowned and carried over the tea, handing one to Liv. "What do you mean?"

"I mean, I'm losing chunks of time I can't account for. I'm closing my eyes one place and waking up in another, and having no memory of moving, or what happened in between."

"Oh, my God, Livvy. That's really worrying."

She chewed at her lower lip. "Yeah, I know."

"Are you sure it's not just alcohol related?"

"That's what I thought the first time. But honestly, it's not as though I really drank that much. Enough for a headache the next day, perhaps, but not complete blackouts. Last thing I remember, it was Friday afternoon, and then when I opened my eyes, you were calling me, and it was one p.m. on Saturday."

"Have you been to the doctor?"

"Not yet. I'm scared of what they'll say. What if it's a brain tumour or something?"

Ellen frowned at her in concern and rubbed her arm again. "Oh, don't say that! I'm sure it's nothing so serious. But you have to get it checked out. You can't just ignore it and hope it stops."

"No?" she said hopefully.

"No!"

What would a doctor say? He'd check she was still taking her medication, that was for sure. Would he order brain scans?

"Do you want me to come with you to the walk-in centre at the hospital?"

Liv waved a hand. "No, I'll book an appointment with the doctor's surgery first thing Monday morning, I promise."

"Do you want me to come with you?

"No, I'll be fine." She didn't want Ellen knowing her medical history. Her friend didn't even know about the antipsychotics she was taking. Maybe they were the problem? She might have been given a bad batch when she'd refilled her prescription after dropping the previous ones into the sink. That would explain it, wouldn't it? They clearly weren't helping at all. Perhaps it would be a good idea to stop taking them, at least until she'd seen the doctor.

Chapter Twenty-two
One Week Earlier

ELLEN STAYED WITH HER for the rest of the day. They ordered in a takeaway and watched endless films on Netflix. Though normally one of the things they'd have done automatically when spending time together was to open a bottle of wine, neither of them mentioned alcohol.

Liv started to feel better as the day went on, but that didn't include the squirming uncertainty that something might have happened during those missing hours. She'd checked her phone to see if she'd drunk called anyone, but there was nothing showing on her call log. But those missing hours haunted her, and she couldn't help thinking back to the previous time when she'd not remembered getting home from her date with Michael, and even the night where Tammy had told her she'd gone out during the night and had left the door open. She'd dismissed it as Tammy being paranoid at the time, but now she started to wonder if it had been her after all.

Ellen tried to convince Liv to call either Michael or Tammy and find out exactly what was happening between them, but the truth was that them having a fling wasn't even what preyed on her mind right now. And she didn't want to be the one chasing them. Michael had called her clingy the last time he'd seen her, and she didn't want to prove him right.

Ellen left to catch the last Tube home, and Liv was faced with a night and the remainder of the weekend alone. She was normally comfortable with her own company, but now she didn't feel right in her own skin. It was as though a silent alarm was sounding inside her head, and she was the only one aware of it.

SHE WOKE SUNDAY MORNING after a restless night, her stomach a tight knot of anxiety. She hadn't been able to eat anything all day in anticipation of Tammy coming home. She would have to say something. She couldn't stand the thought of her flatmate sitting across from her, smug with the knowledge she'd stolen Michael right out from under her nose. Liv knew she and Tammy weren't exactly friends, but she still thought there were moral rules to that kind of thing. Surely your flatmate's boyfriend was off limits. Was that where she'd been all weekend—with Michael? Had there been previous times when Liv had assumed Tammy was out partying when actually she'd been with him?

The thought caused the knot in her stomach to constrict. It was a physical pain, causing her to double over and gasp for breath. Had she thought she was in love with Michael? Love? She wasn't sure she even knew how it felt to be in love, but she'd definitely liked him a lot, and it was the betrayal that was worse than anything.

The hours passed by, and still there was no sign of Tamsin.

Liv couldn't keep going like this. She was driving herself insane.

She picked up her phone for the hundredth time that day, but instead of checking the screen and throwing it back onto the table, she scrolled down to find Michael's name. Her stomach churned with tension. She was almost certain she'd find them together.

Liv pressed the phone to her ear. It only rang twice before he answered.

"Livvy, I'm so pleased you phoned. I've been thinking about you all week."

The jovial tone of his voice threw her.

"What? You have? Why?"

"Because of the way we left things the other day. I meant to call, but then I kept talking myself out of it, telling myself you probably needed some space. I mean, it was all pretty awkward when I was at yours the other day."

She shook her head, baffled, even though she knew he couldn't see her. "It's been a week since I heard from you."

"I know. I'm sorry. I've been swamped with work and house stuff."

"But you've been here since," she snapped.

He hesitated at her change of tone. "Sorry?"

"I saw you here on Friday afternoon. With Tammy."

"Oh, you did? Why didn't you speak to me then?"

"Because I put two and two together. Why else would you be sneaking out of my flat on Friday afternoon?"

"What? Oh, no. That's not it at all. I left my jacket at yours the other night, and I happened to be passing."

"I heard voices—you and Tammy, together."

"Yeah, she was there when I passed by. I told her she should be a little nicer to you, considering ... everything."

"Considering I'm on medication, you mean?" Her heart was pounding, the blood rushing through her ears. "How about *you* being a little nicer to me?"

"What are you talking about? I've only ever been nice to you."

"What, by sleeping with my flatmate, you mean?"

There was silence on the other end. "Liv, I don't know how you've jumped to that conclusion, but that isn't what happened."

"So, where is she now? She's been gone all weekend, and the last person I know who was in her company was you."

"Seriously, Liv. I have no idea. Out clubbing like she does most weekends, I expect."

"And she's still out on a Sunday?"

"Sleeping off a hangover, then? How the hell am I supposed to know? I saw her briefly on Friday, but otherwise I barely know the woman."

"No, you're lying. The two of you are involved, I know you are." A rising panic built inside her, her mind clutching for the truth. He had a way of doing this, of convincing her to think something different. He was playing with her head.

"Liv, you're worrying me. Do you want me to come over?"

"No!" she blurted. "I'll call you if I need you."

She hung up the phone. Michael coming over was the last thing she wanted. If she saw him, he would put thoughts into her head, bend the truth.

She wasn't sure she trusted who she was around him.

Chapter Twenty-three
Five Days Earlier

BY MONDAY MORNING, Tammy still hadn't come home.

Liv was getting worried and called her mobile several times, though it was either switched off or out of battery as it just went straight through to answer phone. It wasn't like Tammy not to come home. However wasted she ended up at the weekend, she always made it back so she'd be ready for work Monday morning.

She'd left enough messages now, and didn't feel she could call any more. How stupid would she feel if Tammy was simply still angry with her, and was staying at someone else's house because she didn't want to be around her? Liv would look like a complete stalker. Tamsin was an adult and was free to do whatever she wanted. She didn't have to report back to Olivia. But something gnawed at her, and she couldn't let it drop.

Liv didn't have any choice but to leave for work just as she did every weekday morning. She couldn't risk losing her job on top of everything else. Even if Tony was a little strange at times, the job was the most stable thing in her life right now, and she desperately needed it.

She arrived at work to an angry client whose buyers had pulled out at the last minute, and another who was being messed around by an incompetent solicitor. Neither of those things were in Liv's control, yet she was the one who caught the brunt of it when the house-sellers needed someone to vent at. At least her being busy meant she didn't have time to mull over everything else that had happened, though she couldn't stop herself from flicking her gaze repeatedly over to her phone, hoping either Tammy or Michael would have called or messaged her. Not that she was really expecting Michael to. After their previous couple of conversations, he probably thought he was better off out of the relationship.

"Hey, how are you after the weekend?" Ellen asked as they stood by the coffee machine.

"No more blackouts, which I guess is a good thing. And I spoke to Michael, and he insists there's nothing going on between him and Tammy, and that he was just popping around to pick up the jacket he'd left there the other day."

A smile of relief spread across Ellen's face. "That's great."

"Yeah, but Tammy didn't come home last night."

The smile vanished. "Oh? Is that normal? She normally stays out a lot, doesn't she?"

"But she's normally home by Sunday night, ready for work the next day. And she's not answering her phone, or replied to any of my texts."

Her lips twisted. "Well, you and Tammy have never exactly been best buddies."

"Maybe not, but I thought she'd at least let me know she's okay. I told her in my messages that I was worried."

Ellen exhaled a sigh. "I'm sure she's fine. She's probably hooked up with some guy and gone straight to work from his place." The smile was back, but this time mischievous. "At least now you know the guy wasn't Michael."

Liv forced a smile in return. "True."

"Honestly, Liv. I think you're being too kind to her. Tammy doesn't give a shit about anyone but herself. I bet you'll get back to the flat and discover her stomping around in a crap mood just like always, and then at least you'll be able to get her to confirm what Michael said about the jacket."

"Yeah, you're probably right."

Ellen gave her a stern look. "And you're going to call the doctor today and make an appointment about the blackouts, right?"

"Yes, I said I would." Quickly, she moved the topic in a different direction. "Anyway, how about you? You're the one who's had this big breakup, and I'm the one hogging all the attention."

Ellen's eyes misted over, her lower lip jutting out, and she glanced away. "He's shut me out of his life completely, so I guess I have to accept it's over. He's going to have to speak to me at some point, though, because I've got a ton of his mail."

The knowledge that she'd gone to see Ryan swirled at her guts. She knew she should tell Ellen everything, but she couldn't bring herself to do it. It would only upset her more, and the truth was that Ellen seemed to be handling things far better than she was right now. Maybe she was being utterly selfish, but she couldn't stand for this to be a new area of animosity in her life. The saying 'don't shoot the messenger' didn't come out of nowhere.

LIV FINISHED UP HER day at work and went home. She still hadn't heard anything from Tammy, and when she let herself into the flat, everything was quiet. She did a quick tour of the place, trying to figure out if there were any clues to show Tammy had been and gone again, but the place looked exactly the same as she'd left it.

She tried her phone again, but once more it went straight through to answer phone.

Taking a seat on the edge of the sofa, she sat holding the phone in her hands and staring at it as though it might have some answers. She'd lived such a separate life from her flatmate that she didn't even know who to contact to see if she'd shown up somewhere else. Tammy told her she was originally from Plymouth, and her dad had buggered off when she was younger, and she didn't really get on with her mother anymore. She worked in marketing for a kitchen company, but that was all Liv really knew. It suddenly occurred to her that Tammy could have hidden as much about her past as Liv had, and neither of them would have been any the wiser.

A sharp knock at the door pulled her from her stupor. Who was knocking? Normally, people used the bell at the main entrance to buzz up. She had the crazy idea that Tammy was home, but why wouldn't she use her key? Unless she'd lost it, of course, or she was hurt and unable to.

Liv got to her feet, her legs loose and wobbly beneath her, and made her way to the door. A peephole embedded into the wood allowed her to see into the hallway, and she leaned into it, squeezing one eye shut so she could get a good look.

Two people, one man and one woman, both around mid-thirties, were standing in the hallway. They looked official, and her chest grew heavy with dread.

Stepping back again, she unlocked the door and pulled it open.

"Olivia Midhurst?" asked the woman.

Liv nodded. "Yes."

"I'm D.C. Flynn, this is D.C. Mayfair. Can we come in?"

She looked anxiously between them. "What's this about?"

"Miss Midhurst, we'd really rather not talk about it in the hall."

She nodded and stepped out of the way, allowing the police officers to step into the flat with her. "Okay, sure." Immediately, guilt swamped her, and her gaze darted over everything she could see in the flat, hoping there was nothing incriminating. Sometimes Tammy liked to smoke a little weed in the evenings, and Liv would just about die of mortification if the police officers noticed some remnants of it on the coffee table.

"Please, have a seat." She gestured to the sofa, relieved she couldn't see anything illegal lying around.

Both officers sat awkwardly side by side, perched right at the edge. The woman had a folder of notes, which she placed on her knees.

"This is the known address of Miss Tamsin Ashe?" asked the male half, D.C. Mayfair.

"Yes, that's right. She's my flatmate." Liv looked anxiously between the police officers, her hands clutched together in her lap. "Is she okay?"

"I hate to be the one to have to tell you this, but I'm afraid she's not. Her body was recovered from a park earlier today."

Liv froze, her mind pulling away at the edges. She reached out and grabbed the armrests of the chair, trying to steady herself.

"What?" Her voice sounded distant, like it didn't belong to her at all.

"We're not treating her death as suspicious at this time."

Liv blinked. "How can it not be suspicious? She's dead!"

"It would seem she sent some friends and family a number of concerning text messages before she died."

She shook her head. "I don't understand. What are you trying to say?"

"We believe Tamsin may have taken her own life."

She barked sudden and inappropriate laughter. "Tammy? Kill herself? No way."

The female officer frowned. "What makes you so certain?"

"That just isn't who Tammy is … was … I mean. She's confident, and beautiful, and got everything going for her. She wouldn't do something like that."

The officer's tone softened. "Quite often it is the ones we suspect the least who are going through the hardest battles. They have a way of hiding how they're feeling from everyone around them."

What she said was true—Liv knew that better than most. But she still didn't believe Tammy had killed herself.

Michael.

Other than her, he was the last one to see Tamsin. She suddenly remembered the blonde woman who had turned up dead, too. Hadn't they said she'd also killed herself? It was too much of a coincidence, surely, for the deaths not to be linked.

Liv opened her mouth to say something, and then snapped it shut again. She'd be throwing Michael into the lion's den, and possibly for no reason, if she said something. He would never forgive her if she told the police she thought he could be involved in the deaths of two young women. The cops thought both deaths were suicide. They were professionals. They must have good reason for thinking such a thing.

"How ..." Her voice broke, and she cleared her throat, composing herself. She tried again. "How did she do it?"

"It was a drugs overdose," D.C. Mayfair, the male half of the duo, said. "Cocaine. We believe she has a history of drug abuse, which probably led to her mentally fragile state."

Liv shook her head. "She was a party girl, that was all. It was recreational. It's not as though she was sitting on the street doing it."

The woman officer frowned slightly at her, obviously reading the myriad of expressions flitting across Liv's face. "Is there something you'd like to tell us? Something you've thought of?"

"Oh, no, not really."

"When was the last time you saw Tamsin alive?"

She could tell her now, that it had been when she'd come home early and seen Michael leaving, shortly followed by Tammy. But if she did, they'd question Michael, and they'd want to know why they'd all argued, and then the medication she was on was bound to be brought up, and if that was mentioned, they'd be sure to look into her past. It was a can of worms she didn't want to open.

If Tammy had killed herself, Liv wouldn't be helping anyone by bringing all that up. She'd only be causing trouble for all those left behind.

"When she left for work Friday morning," she said instead. "She didn't seem any different than any other day."

The officer gave a tight smile and snapped her notebook shut. "Okay." She reached out, and Liv saw she was holding something out to her. It was a business card. "If you think of anything at all that might be of interest to us, please, do call."

She took the card. "I will."

The officers got to their feet, and Liv showed them to the door. They both gave her polite smiles as they stepped out into the hallway, and Liv gently closed the door on them.

Her limbs trembled, her hands shaking and her legs weak. An empty chasm had appeared where her stomach used to be. She managed to get back over to the couch and sank down onto the cushions. In shock, she covered her mouth with her hand. Tammy, dead? She struggled to even think of it. How can someone who had been walking around the flat only days before now simply no longer exist?

She needed to see Michael and find out what was said between him and Tammy when he last saw her. Did he say something to her that made her do what she had? The possibility seemed crazy, but she had to know, if only to put her own mind to rest.

Liv found her phone, and her trembling hand caused her to misdial, but then she pulled up his number and swiped the screen to call him. He answered after the second ring, as though he'd been waiting for her to call.

"Liv," he said, his tone serious. "Is everything okay?"

That simple question caused her to burst into tears. "No. No, it's not. Nothing is okay," she managed to say between choked, hitching breaths.

"Why? What's happened?"

"It's Tammy," she blurted. "She's dead."

"What?" The word was a snapped syllable.

Liv stifled a sob, her knuckles pressed against her mouth. "The police were just here. They think she killed herself."

"God, that's awful. Are you all right?"

"No, I'm not. I need to see you."

He hesitated, and then said, "Are you at home?"

"Yes."

"I'll be there in half an hour."

The line went dead.

Liv put her head in her hands. She was caught in a nightmare, and she didn't know how to escape. She wanted someone to tell her this was all a mistake, and they'd wrongly identified the body. Tammy might never have been her favourite person, but she never would have wanted her dead. Was she really going through the sort of depression that would cause someone to take their own life? Liv knew that kind of depression—she'd skated on the edges of it many times before—and it was intense and solitary and often messy. But maybe Tammy had hidden it well. She had seemed her usual self when she'd left the flat on Friday afternoon. Liv had assumed that was because she'd just spent the previous hour or so fucking her boyfriend, but Michael had promised her that hadn't been the case. But then what had she been doing at the flat? She should have been working that afternoon. Had she called in sick? Was this something the police had looked into?

Liv hadn't moved from her spot on the couch and was surprised when the buzzer to the door sounded. She'd lost track of time, so caught up in her thoughts. The sound immediately sent her stomach rolling like the inside of a washing machine. What was she going to say to him? Did she truly believe he might be connected in the deaths of two women? And, if she was, should she even be alone with him right now?

If they did it to themselves, how could Michael possibly be involved? The police didn't think there was anything suspicious going on.

Yes, but the police didn't know about the connection between Tammy and Holly Newie—if Holly was even the same girl she'd seen Michael arguing with. Michael said he didn't think it was, and if it wasn't, then there was no connection, and she was drawing lines where there weren't any.

The buzzer went again, insistent. She couldn't leave him standing outside when she'd basically invited him over.

Her legs felt like rubber, her bowels weak and watery, as she made her way over to the door and hit the button to let him up. She waited until she heard the lift coming to a halt on her floor, and then opened the door.

Michael stepped out, his handsome face pinched in concern. In her head, she started to imagine him as some kind of monster who was wandering around driving women to do unspeakable things, but now he was here, she saw it was only him—the man she'd grown to know and care about over the last month.

He caught her eye and offered her a sympathetic smile. "Hey," he said softly.

"Hi," she replied, suddenly choked with emotion.

He pulled her in and hugged her tight. She froze in his grip, still caught up in a whirlwind of confusion, making no effort to hold him back.

He must have figured out her body language and untangled himself from her. "What's wrong?"

She couldn't talk about this in the middle of the hall. She grabbed his hand and tugged him inside the flat and shut the door behind them.

Liv turned to face him. "As far as I know, you were the last one to see Tammy alive."

He frowned, shaking his head. "I saw her briefly when I came to get my jacket. That was all."

"What was she doing here?"

His frown deepened. "What?"

"She should have been at work, but she was here, with you. Why?"

He shrugged. "I have no idea. She didn't say."

"But you knew someone was here in order for you to pick up the jacket, and you never called me."

"I called the landline, and Tammy picked up. I wasn't going to start questioning why she was in her own flat."

"You were arguing with her. I heard you from outside."

"I already explained that to you. I told her that her behaviour the other day was out of order." He huffed out a breath of exasperation. "What is this? A fucking inquisition?"

She jammed her hands on her hips and tried to hold her nerve. He was too good at breaking her down, of making her do what he wanted. Was that what he'd done with Holly Newie and Tamsin, too? Had he somehow convinced them to hurt themselves?

"I'm allowed to ask questions, Michael. It would be strange if I wasn't questioning what happened. Try to see things from my point of view. Tammy started an argument between us a week ago, and then I don't see or hear from you—"

He cut her off, pointing a finger at her. "I didn't see or hear from you either, Liv. Don't make out like this is all one-sided. You could have easily picked up the phone, too."

He was trying to turn the conversation away from Tammy, but she wouldn't let him. "And then I catch you here at the flat with her, and the next thing I know she's dead. Now, you're telling me that was all completely unconnected."

His eyes narrowed, a muscle twitching in his jaw. "I hope you didn't say any of this to the police."

"Why? What have you got to hide?"

"Nothing! But the last thing I need right now is the police poking around. You think I want to be associated with a young woman's death? You know how bad that will look? Jesus, Liv, sometimes I don't think you live in the real world."

She burst into tears again, turning her face and angling her body away from him.

"Oh, Livvy. I'm sorry. I'm so sorry. I'm being an insensitive arse." He caught hold of her arm and pulled her back around. "Come here."

This time, when he tugged her in to hold her, she let him. She needed that confirmation of life, of touch and comfort. His strong arms wrapped around her, and she pressed her face to his chest, crying into his t-shirt. He was warm and smelled so good, and she clung to his back, rumpling the material of his shirt between her fists like a baby with a comforter.

When her tears subsided, she lifted her face from his chest. Her cheeks burned with humiliation at her show of emotion, and she looked away. But his touch under her chin lifted her face to his, and he kissed away her tears. The feel of his mouth on hers helped to soften away all the sharp edges of anxiety that had been slicing her to pieces all week. This was just Michael. There was no reason to think his explanation of things weren't the correct ones. Tammy probably saw a ton of people after she'd seen Michael at the flat, and the people Tammy hung out with weren't exactly the naïve, innocent types either.

His hands tangled in her hair as their kisses grew deeper and more frantic. She pressed herself up against the hard planes of his body, wanting him to make her forget everything else. He could make her feel good, could calm her racing mind, and she needed that right now. He reached under her bottom and lifted her, her legs wrapping around his hips as he carried her into the bedroom. They dropped to the bed, with her still straddling him. His hardness pressed against the intimate spot between her thighs, and she gasped, grinding harder. Their breathing came ragged, their tongues lashing. Hair was pulled, bite marks left on skin, as though they were both pleasuring and punishing each other at the same time.

She felt as though she was sinking and he was the life raft for her to cling onto. Because that was what a drowning person did. Even if the raft was full of holes and coming to pieces at the edges, if that was all you had, you still clutched it tight and prayed it would save you.

Chapter Twenty-four
Four Days Earlier

MICHAEL STAYED THE whole night.

The following morning, he made them both coffee, and then kissed her as he left for work, almost as though they were a regular couple. Only the empty bedroom across the hall where her flatmate should have been sleeping was like a vast, empty chasm, sucking all positive thought from Liv's head and swallowing it whole.

She did her best to feel happy about Michael, but it was impossible to be happy about anything when Tammy's young life had been cut so short. Had she really been so unhappy? A horrible part of Liv wondered if there was more she could have done. After all, she'd spent the previous week ignoring Tammy. Had she made things worse? Had *she* actually been the reason Tammy had taken an overdose? But Tammy had been the one to start that fight, and it wasn't as though she'd acted like she'd cared. If anything, Tammy acted as though she got a kick out of the argument, like a part of her had enjoyed trying to rip Liv's relationship to shreds. Liv had never wanted Tammy to tell Michael about her meds, but at least now it was out in the open. He didn't know all of her past, and she hoped he never would, but—as much as Tammy's heart hadn't been in the right place—she'd been right when she'd said she'd saved Liv that awkward conversation.

When Olivia got to work, she went straight to Tony's office to tell him what had happened. He needed to know the reason she seemed upset at work, and there was even the chance the police might stop by with more questions. Either way, it seemed like the right thing to do. She needed to tell Ellen as well. Ellen hadn't known Tammy well, but they were acquaintances, and this kind of thing always came as a shock.

"Take some time off, if you need it," Tony told her. "This must all be terribly upsetting for you."

But she shook her head. "I'd rather be here, staying busy, than home in an empty flat. Everywhere I look, I see memories of her. I don't believe in ghosts, but I can kind of understand why people might feel like they're seeing one."

"Of course. Whatever you need."

"Thanks, Tony."

He was a good man. She'd been unfair to him. A twinge of guilt went though her at laughing over him and his fruit basket with Michael. He'd been trying to be nice, and she hadn't appreciated him at all.

"What's going on?" Ellen hissed at her as she came out of the office.

Liv pressed her lips together and caught Ellen's arm to pull her away. She didn't want to be the talk of the office. A couple of the others had met Tammy, but only in passing. She knew word would get around quickly enough that her flatmate had died, but for the moment she was happier if it was as few as possible.

"Let's go and grab a coffee."

She caught Tony's eye through the window dividing his office from the rest of their desks and pointed towards the door to show she was going out. He'd just told her to take time, if she needed it, so she was sure he wouldn't mind her stealing Ellen for half an hour.

The two women left the building.

"Tell me what's going on?" Ellen insisted when they got outside.

Liv found herself blinking back tears again. "It's Tammy. She killed herself at the weekend."

Ellen's eyebrows shot up her forehead. "What? How? Why?"

She shook her head. "I don't know. The police say it was an overdose, but I can't believe she'd do something like that on purpose. She just wasn't like that."

Ellen clutched her hand to her mouth. "Jesus Christ. So you were right to worry about her not coming home. I'm so sorry." She must have thought of something else. "Didn't you say Michael was there with her on Friday afternoon? And then she shows up dead?"

Liv could see where Ellen's train of thought was going. She didn't blame her—after all, hadn't she thought exactly the same thing?

"Michael didn't have anything to do with it, Elles. I've already spoken to him. In fact, he stayed over last night because I didn't want to be on my own."

If such a thing was possible, Ellen's mouth dropped even further. "You were in the flat with him on your own all of last night. Fucking hell, Liv. Why didn't you call me? No one else knew the two of you were together. What if he had something to do with Tammy killing herself, and then he tried something with you? None of us would be any the wiser."

A bubble of irritation rose inside her. "He explained everything. He just called around to pick up his jacket, that's all. He barely knew Tammy."

"I'm worried about you being around him, Liv. What if he's dangerous?"

She gave a small, cold laugh. "He's not dangerous."

"No? What do you really know about this guy?"

"I know enough. I know what he does for a living, and what he likes to read and what music he listens to. I know how he likes his steak cooked and that he doesn't take sugar in his tea."

She lifted her eyebrows. "Is that enough?"

"Well, how much do we ever really know about another person?" She couldn't help her mind going to her own situation. In truth, Ellen knew far less about Liv than Liv did about Michael.

Ellen pressed her lips together and shook her head. "I don't know, sweetie. I'm just worried about you. You know I got a bad feeling about him that first time we met, and now with all this other stuff coming up ... You can't honestly say you feel one hundred percent happy with all of this either."

"I don't feel happy with it at all," she admitted.

"So, take a step back. Have some space, at least. Tammy's death is a huge shock, even if the two of you weren't close. The last thing you need is the worry that Michael might have been involved."

"I don't really think that," she interrupted. "Please don't think that. I would go to the police if I believed he was involved in any way. I just wish I hadn't seen him coming out of the flat that day."

She reached out and squeezed Liv's hand. "It's better that you know. At least this way you can make a decision with your eyes open. But I really do think you should keep away from Michael for a little while. You haven't been quite right since you met him, and now with what's happened with Tammy ..." She trailed off and shrugged. "I just think you should put some space between you, that's all."

She didn't like what Ellen was saying. Perhaps it was because so many of her words were echoing her own thoughts from the previous night when she'd confronted Michael. But she'd put that behind her. She and Michael had slept together again, and he'd promised her he had nothing to do with Tammy killing herself, or Holly Newie, who Ellen didn't even know about. But still she felt her defences rise.

"You've never liked Michael, so I don't expect you to take his side now."

"Hey, this isn't about sides. I'm on *your* side. I always will be."

Her hackles had risen, and she shook her head. "No, you'd be happier if Michael and I weren't together. It would mean you wouldn't feel so bad about not having Ryan around now."

Something in Ellen's blue eyes hardened. "At least I haven't chased Ryan around. At least I knew who he was before I got so involved with him."

She snorted laughter, but it contained no humour. "Oh, yeah. Ryan. The perfect man you were always lording over the rest of us. Didn't turn out so perfect when he went and got his twenty-one year old colleague knocked up, though." The words were out of her mouth before she'd even realised she was going to say them. Of course, Ellen didn't know yet. She'd never told her.

Or at least, she *hadn't* known, because she certainly knew now.

The blood drained from her friend's face. "What did you just say?"

"I'm sorry, Elles," she said in horror, reaching out for her hand, but Ellen jerked it away. "I didn't mean that."

"Ryan's got a twenty-one year old pregnant?"

"I'm sorry ..."

"Tell me the truth, Olivia," she snapped.

Liv had never seen her like this—sharp, and hard, and direct. "I went to see him when he finished work. He told me then."

"He told you he'd got another woman pregnant?"

"Not in so many words, but he said she wasn't there because she had an appointment, and he didn't deny it when I jumped to the conclusion she was pregnant. This other woman, Sierra, gave him an ultimatum, and he chose her. I'm so sorry."

Ellen was backing away, shaking her head. "I have to go. Tell Tony I've come down with something, okay?"

"Of course, but are you going to be all right?" She desperately wished she was able to take her words back. That had been her fault. She'd been angry, and the last person she should ever hurt was Ellen.

Chapter Twenty-five
Present Day

THE BLOW FROM HIS BOOT caught her smack in the face, sending her flying backwards. Pain exploded through her nose. She slammed into the floor, her head smacking against the hard concrete with an impossibly loud crack that sounded as though it had happened right inside her head. The impact jolted through her bones, her teeth snapping shut, catching the side of her tongue. Fireworks burst behind her eyes, and her mind spun in a slow, dizzying circle. All she could taste was blood, thick and cloying, as it ran down the back of her throat, making her choke.

She lay there, unable to move. The pain in her face was so overwhelming, her body didn't seem to be able to process anything else. Her vision flashed with bright white sparks, as though she'd been staring at the sun for too long, or had caught the flash of a camera. For a moment, she even forgot where she was, and her situation. All she could do was try to get her body to start processing things again, instead of being muted by the pain.

Broken. Her nose must be broken. Her entire face throbbed with the rhythm of her pulse. The blood continued to flow, spilling down her face and running down the back of her throat. She was lying on her back, and she knew she needed to move if she didn't want to choke to death on her own blood. Had a person ever died of a broken nose before? The idea seemed ridiculous, but it wasn't just the kick to the face that had left her stunned, it was also the impact of the back of her head against the concrete floor. Now she knew how he'd felt when she'd hit him with the bottle.

Fuck.

Realisation jolted through her, sending a fresh spurt of adrenaline through her veins. When he'd kicked her, one of his hands had been loosened from the rope. He was most likely working that hand free right now, and the second it was loose, he'd be able to pull the gag out of his mouth.

Terror coursed through her system in equal measure to the pain. Was this it? Had she lost? After everything she'd been through, this would be the end. What would he make her do? The same as the others, or would he ensure it was even worse to punish her for what she'd done to him? She'd never find out her location either—another innocent left to die.

A sob bubbled up inside her, but it came out of her mouth as a groan.

Move! A voice inside her head commanded. *You've got to move!*

This wasn't over yet. He wasn't free.

She couldn't let him win, not after everything. He wouldn't get his hand free right away. It would take time, which meant *she* still had time. All she needed to do was force herself to her feet and get back over to him. If she could tighten the knot before he freed himself, things would go back to the way they'd been before she'd made such a stupid mistake.

Except if he can't write, then you'll have no way of getting him to tell you the truth. She couldn't risk getting that close to him again to hold up the notepad, or loosen his hand enough to hold a pen. *Plus, you have a broken nose and are bleeding all over the damn place.*

But the possibility of securing him again was enough to get her moving. She rolled onto her stomach and somehow managed to push herself to all fours. Her head felt like a dead weight, hanging from her neck, as though her skull had been filled with concrete. Blood dripped from her face and onto the floor below. She blinked hard, trying to clear her vision. *Come on, move faster,* the voice in her head urged her on, but she struggled to get her body to comply.

The grunts and laboured breathing of him trying to escape came from behind her. Like her, he must have known time was running out. He'd want to get free before she came back to her senses.

With monumental effort, she managed to get one foot flat on the floor, and then the second, so she ended up in a strange, bloodied, downward dog position. From there, her hands went to her thighs, and she straightened.

The change in position only made her face throb more, and she was forced to hold still for a moment as the room spun around her.

Her equilibrium returned, and she wiped the blood from her eyes and turned to face him.

He still hung from the hook in the ceiling. He hadn't yet managed to free himself. His right hand was almost loose, however, the fingers bunched in together as the tight loop of rope squeezed up his hand. He saw that she was back on her feet, and his eyes widened, his struggles renewing with fresh urgency.

"Oh, no, you don't." Her voice was a low growl, rattling with congealed blood. It didn't sound like her at all.

The man yelled against the gag, the sound coming out muffled, and he refocused on his hand. The rope was almost off now, squeezing his thumb and finger together, making the circumference as small as possible so he could pull it out of the loop.

"No!"

She lunged for him. She needed to push the circle of rope back down his wrist and pull the knot tight around it.

But he was ready for her this time. As soon as she got close enough, he swung out his elbow, trying to catch her in the face. Loosening his hand had given him the extra movement he needed, where before his arm had been stretched too straight to give him room.

They were both suffering—both impaired by the injuries they had given each other. Reactions had slowed, and she hadn't anticipated the movement. But she was shorter than him, and even while standing on her tiptoes, grappling to reach the rope, his elbow was still higher than her face. It skimmed the top of her head, but his bicep delivered where his elbow had failed, shoving her backwards.

She staggered back, barely managing to stay on her feet. The floor was covered in her blood, and though the blood loss seemed to have slowed for the moment, it made the polished concrete slippery. Her feet went out from under her, and she slammed back down on her hands and knees.

Lifting her head back up, ignoring the pain, she watched in horror as he gave a final muffled roar of determination and yanked his hand through the rest of the rope bonds.

His hand was free.

Chapter Twenty-six
Three Days earlier

LIV HAD NEVER FELT so alone.

It was as though she was going through the motions of her life, without actually taking part. There was a screen between her and the real world, and she didn't know how to break through it. Ellen wasn't speaking to her. The only person she had was Michael, and she wasn't sure she could trust who she was with him.

It was strange being in the flat, but she didn't know where else to go. Everywhere she looked, she saw Tammy's belongings. What would happen to them? She guessed Tammy's mum would send for them at some point, but that was probably the least of their concerns right now. The poor woman must be reeling in shock and grief. Liv wished she had some way of contacting her, to tell her how sorry she was, and ask if there was anything else she could do—box up some of her stuff, perhaps. But she didn't want it to look as though she was trying to get rid of Tammy's belongings. She could always look through her things and see if there was an address book or something else that might have her family's contact details, but even with Tammy dead, it felt wrong to rifle through her private things.

At some point, she'd need to think about all the practical side of things as well, about how she no longer had a flatmate to split the rent and bills with. There was no way she could afford this place on her own—she'd go broke within a couple of months—and even if she could afford it, the atmosphere in the flat was haunted now, and she wasn't sure that was something she'd ever get over.

Michael came over after work. She didn't really want him there, but she couldn't bring herself to ask him to leave. Everything Ellen had said was playing on her mind, and she wanted some space to process what had happened.

He came up behind her as she stirred pasta sauce on the stove. His arm wrapped around her waist, and he planted a kiss on the side of her neck. But she froze at his contact, and he pulled away.

"What's wrong?"

She didn't want to tell him, worried he'd hate Ellen for it, and things would get even more awkward between them all when they made up, but, as always when she was around Michael, she couldn't seem to help herself.

"You mean other than my flatmate apparently killing herself a few days ago?" Her voice was laced in bitterness.

Michael pressed his lips together and folded his arms across his chest. "You know what I'm asking, Olivia."

"Ellen and I had a fight," she admitted reluctantly.

"Oh? What about?"

"You. She thinks there's something off about you, and she thinks I should put some distance between us."

She hated the way the words came tripping off her tongue. It was as though all he needed was to fix her in that dark gaze and command her to tell him, and she'd have no choice but to do it. She'd seen him do that same thing to others—like when that man had tried to take the black cab. All it had taken was a few words from Michael, and the other man had backed right off. She didn't know how he managed to do that.

His eyes narrowed. "She thinks you should put some distance between us? Who the hell does she think she is, trying to come between us? Just because her relationship failed doesn't mean she has to destroy yours, too."

"She's not trying to destroy us."

"Yeah, right. Misery loves company, isn't that what they say? She just wants you all to herself. How about we turn this around on her and we make it so she's the one who needs some distance?"

Prickles of unease crawled up Liv's arms. "What are you saying?"

"You should stay away from Ellen. She's bad news."

Liv shook her head. "No, she's my best friend. She's my only real friend."

"She's no good for you. Stay away from her."

She could feel the intensity of his gaze, how he always locked her in his dark stare and then told her exactly what he wanted her to do. She felt it now, something deep inside her pushing her to agree with what he wanted.

Behind her, the pasta sauce was starting to burn, and she reached back and turned off the stove.

"I think we should stop seeing each other." The words came out of nowhere, her heart beating so hard it made her lightheaded and nauseated. "This isn't working out."

His expression grew tight, as though the muscles in his cheeks, jaw, and forehead might pop out of his skin. "What?"

His dark eyes focused on her, and she took another hitching breath.

"I don't think we should see each other again," she forced herself to say.

His upper lip curled, and he slowly shook his head. "No."

"No? What do you mean, 'no?'"

"You don't get to finish with me."

"Yes, yes, I do." She had to stick to her guns, but she felt him drawing her in.

"That would be a mistake, Olivia. Is this just because of what Ellen said? You're allowed to have two separate worlds, you know. Before this, I never told you to stay away from your friends, but they're allowed to tell you to stay away from me? Doesn't that make them the bad ones? The controlling ones?"

You just did tell me to stay away from Ellen, she thought but didn't say.

"I don't know." She shook her head. "This is all too much. I just need some space."

He stepped in, and she reared back, but he took her chin in his fingers and lifted her face to his. "Tell me you don't mean it."

"What?" She was frozen in his grasp.

"Tell me you don't want us to break up."

He'd locked her in his stare again, and she could feel the urge to give in to what he wanted. She fought to keep her tongue still and not allow him to influence what she did and thought. Because that was exactly what he was doing. She didn't know how—if it was a kind of hypnosis or something else—but he was making her do and say things she didn't want to.

"How do you do that?" she said, staring up at him, his face swimming through her unshed tears. She'd heard of songs that got stuck in your head referred to as ear worms. That was what Michael's voice was like. An ear worm that drilled into her brain until she had no choice but to give in or lose her mind.

"Do what?"

"I don't know. You suggest things and they just feel right to me, even though I was thinking the exact opposite only moments before."

"I don't know. Maybe you simply don't have much conviction in your own thoughts."

She yanked her chin out of his grip. "But I do! With anyone else, I do. But then I come up against you, and it's like I can't hold my own thoughts in my head. You tell me something, and I just believe it, or do it."

"Perhaps you need to be a little stronger."

Her chest swelled with righteous indignation. "This has nothing to do with me. This is something you're doing!"

A small line appeared beneath his brows. "Do you really believe that, Livvy? Do you know how insane that sounds?"

A horrific thought entered her head. "Did you do something to Tammy and that other woman? Did you tell them to do something to themselves?"

"Yeah, I told them to go kill themselves, and they did it." His tone was filled with sarcasm, but she knew it hid the truth. "Not everyone is as suggestible as you, Livvy."

"Fuck you!"

He grabbed her arm, staring hard into her eyes. Liv squeezed her eyes shut, but she knew it wasn't enough. The way he captured her in his gaze was only a part of what he did. It was his words that conjured the magic, that wove their way into her brain and played over and over and over until she eventually gave in to them. It was the only way to silence his voice—by doing what he wanted. Was that how the other women felt—Holly Newie and Tammy, too? Did he tell them to hurt themselves until they eventually gave in and did it?

"Maybe you're the one who should have killed herself," he spat.

She stared at him, unable to believe what she'd just heard. "What?"

The handsome, charismatic man she'd known had vanished. His face was contorted into a slash of anger and hatred. "You heard me. Stupid bitch like you. You're worthless. Thinking you're better than me. Acting all suspicious just because I happened to drop in and pick up a jacket. Are you even hearing yourself? You're insane. Those pills you take clearly aren't doing the job. Put an end to your misery and finish it for the good of all of us. No wonder your flatmate killed herself. She probably couldn't stand to be around you any longer."

Liv snatched her hands out of his grasp, but the damage was already done. He shot her a final look of disgust before he turned and stormed from the flat.

But his words stayed with her.
Kill yourself.
Put an end to your misery.
Finish it.

Over and over they rolled in her head, until she was unable to think anything else. Tears seeped from the corners of her eyes, spilling down her face. *No, no, no.* Was this how he did it? How he'd got rid of the other two? Had he told Tammy the same thing when he'd been here on Friday, and she'd been compelled to take her own life?

She knew thinking such a thing was crazy, yet the words continued to work their way into her head. He had a kind of power over others, and she wasn't strong enough to defend herself against it.

He was right, and he didn't even know about her past, about the terrible thing she'd done. She brought nothing to this world.

With her thoughts a cyclone inside her head, her feet took her to the bathroom. It would all be over then. The idea of sweet nothingness felt like bliss. Just for it all to end. All the running and the fighting. It wasn't as though she hadn't contemplated it before. There had been plenty of times when she'd thought it would be for the best, and now here she was again. A full circle.

Thoughts of Michael went from her mind. Instead, these were her thoughts now, her ideas. How should she do it? Tablets? She had plenty of pills, including some strong sleeping tablets. But she knew the chance of throwing them all up before they'd done the job was high.

Disposable razors caught her eye in her medicine cabinet. She could smash one open, and cut, cut, cut. Yes, that seemed right to her, somehow. It balanced things within her, calming her mind. She deserved to be punished for everything, and for that punishment to be at her own hands resonated with her.

That didn't stop her hand from trembling as she reached into the medicine cabinet and took down the razor. It was brand new, the piece of clear plastic still covering the blades for protection. She slipped the piece of plastic off and let it drop into the sink then looked around for something to smash the head of the razor. Her toothbrush holder was a grey marble pot and should be heavy enough. She flung the toothbrush to one side—it wasn't as though she'd need it again—and placed the disposable razor face up on the side of the sink. With the toothbrush holder in one hand, holding the end of the razor steady in the other, she brought the marble pot down hard. The plastic cracked, the vibration travelling up her arm, but it wasn't enough. With teeth gritted, she brought the pot down again and again, slamming the marble into the plastic and metal until the plastic was no more than fragmented pieces and the slivers of razorblades lay discarded between them.

Liv's heart caught and her eyes filled with tears as she pushed the pieces of shattered plastic to one side and picked up one of the blades. When she thought of everything that had happened, it seemed only right that things would end like this. What was the point in her keeping going? She was all alone now—she'd even managed to drive her best friend away because of her short temper and loose tongue. No one was going to miss her when she was gone. Everyone would continue with their lives, regardless.

Though she knew it was the right thing to do, that didn't stop misery and regret filling her soul. She blinked back tears, and sniffed, and brought the sharp edge of the blade to the skin of her inner wrist. It was going to hurt, but she deserved that, too. After all the pain she'd caused other people, it was only right that the last thing she experienced was anguish herself.

Liv dug her teeth into her lower lip, squeezed her eyes shut so she didn't have to watch what she was doing, and brought the blade across her skin.

Chapter Twenty-seven
Three Days Earlier

"SHE'S COMING ROUND."

A strange voice filtered through to her ears. A male voice.

What was a strange man doing in her flat? Her eyes were still shut, and the lids felt as though they'd been weighted down so she couldn't quite open them. What had happened? Was she in her bedroom? The surface beneath her body felt cold and hard, and not like her bed at all. Had she suffered another blackout? Had she been drinking too much again?

"Oh, Livvy. Thank God." She recognised Ellen's voice.

Her mind raced, trying to put the pieces of what had happened back together again. Why was Ellen here?

Someone started to put something over her face, and the action was enough to bring her round fully. Her eyes shot open, and she pushed away at the thing trying to cover her face.

"Calm down," the male voice said again. "It's okay. My name is Stephen, and I'm a paramedic. This is just to give you a little extra oxygen."

She suddenly became aware of the pain in her arms, and it all came flooding back to her. The man speaking to her was here to help, and there was someone else wearing the same uniform standing behind him. But how had they known what she'd done?

"We're going to take you in," he said, his voice calm, "get you checked out."

Her stomach lurched at the idea of going into hospital.

She pushed the oxygen mask away again, needing to speak. When she lifted her arm, the lower half was swaddled in thick white bandages. "No, no. I'm fine. I'm okay."

"You have some serious lacerations to your wrists. They may need stitches, so I'm afraid we're going to have to insist."

Her gaze sought Ellen's. Her friend stood on the other side of her, her fingers to her mouth, her face filled with concern. "I'm okay, Ellen. I don't need to go to hospital."

"You tried to hurt yourself, Liv."

"I don't understand. How did you know?"

"I got scared when you weren't answering, and came over."

She tried to sit up straighter. "You what?"

"It's okay. The front door was unlocked, and I found you in here. I was worried after you weren't answering your phone, and after what happened with Tammy ... I couldn't take any risks."

She was still putting together the events leading up to this moment. Now she was coming around fully, she was able to take in her surroundings. There was blood. Too much blood. Surely that couldn't have all come from her? It was streaked across the tiles and the sink and the floor. Red smeared over her clothes and across her skin. She spotted the smashed disposable razor. She'd done what she'd planned, so why hadn't it worked? Would she be dead right now if Ellen hadn't interfered?

You didn't want to die.

A stretcher was brought in, and the paramedics lifted her up and onto it. They'd already bandaged her wrists when she'd been unconscious to stop the bleeding, so she couldn't see how bad the cuts were. But she was alive, so she knew she hadn't done that good a job.

"I can walk," she insisted.

The male paramedic shook his head. "Sorry, ambulance rules."

"Where are you taking me?"

"Accident and Emergency."

"It's okay, Livvy," Ellen said. "I'm coming with you."

Ellen stayed beside the stretcher as she was carried out of the flat and down the stairs to the waiting ambulance outside. Liv cringed down, hating the stares of the passers-by, all trying to catch a glimpse of what had happened. She felt small and pathetic. She had done this to herself.

No, you didn't. Michael did this to you, remember? He made you do it.

Yes, that was right. It was starting to come back to her. Michael had used that ability of his to tell her to hurt herself, and she hadn't been able to stop the events he'd put into motion. Had he said something similar to Tammy when she'd overheard them fighting that day at the flat? Had he even told Holly Newie to go and throw herself off a cliff?

Liv's mind blurred. What she was contemplating was insane. She knew exactly how it sounded. And with her history, no one would believe her. In fact, after this latest incident, they'd probably use it as more proof that she was unstable, and then she wouldn't be released, and Michael would be out there, doing whatever the hell he wanted to the next person who upset him.

She was bundled into the back of the ambulance, Ellen climbing in with her. The sirens went on, and within minutes they were at the Accident and Emergency department.

Liv was embarrassed. This was too much fuss for her. She felt a bit dizzy, and her left arm was throbbing, but otherwise she didn't think she needed medical attention. She was taken into a bay and transferred from the gurney onto a bed.

"Someone will be around to see you shortly," the nurse who'd taken over from the paramedics told her. "Try to relax until then."

"Am I allowed to stay?" Ellen asked her.

"Yes, that's fine," the nurse said with a reassuring smile. "Just try to let her get some rest."

Ellen found a plastic seat and pulled it up alongside the bed. They were sharing the medical bay with a number of other patients, but everyone seemed to be ignoring each other.

"How did you find me?" she asked Ellen again, wanting to know every detail of what had happened to this point.

Ellen leaned out and held her hand. "I was worried about you after our fight. I called you and then the flat's landline, and got no response. When I came round, the door wasn't locked, so I just let myself in and found you like that. Perhaps I overreacted by calling the ambulance, but after everything that had happened with Tammy, I was worried. Why did you do it, Livvy? Why did you hurt yourself like that?"

"I didn't." Fresh tears filled her eyes, and the hospital ward swam around her. "It was Michael."

Ellen's eyes widened in horror. "What? Michael cut you like this?"

"No, but he made me do it. He told me to hurt myself, and I did. That's what he does. I think he told another woman to hurt herself as well. She was called Holly Newie, and she vanished the other week and then turned up dead. I thought I saw them arguing a few weeks ago. And he got to Tammy, too. They didn't kill themselves because they wanted to. They killed themselves because he made them."

"Liv, do you know what that sounds like? Michael can't have made them kill themselves."

"He did. I don't know how. It's like he has this power of suggestion. He's done it to me so many times, making me do things I wouldn't normally. I don't know if he's a hypnotist, or if it's some kind of magic, but it's what he does, Ellen!" Her voice grew high pitched with panic.

"Okay, you need to calm down."

"I can't. Don't you see? He thinks he's dealt with me. What happens when he realises it didn't work? He'll come back for me, I'm sure he will." She tightened her fingers around Ellen's. "I'm frightened of him."

Ellen's lips were pressed together, her nostrils flared as she shook her head. "That son-of-a-bitch."

"Please, don't go near him. He's dangerous."

"We have to tell the police."

"No, please, no police." She didn't want them to look into her background, knowing how it would appear. They'd find out about her past. Plus, what could she say—that she thought Michael had an ability to tell people what to do, and they just did it? She'd be laughed out of the station. No, worse than that.

They'd assume she was ill again, and she'd end up back in that place. "Please, Ellen. Just leave it. No one is going to believe me."

Ellen's eyes were fixed on her face, searching hers, and Liv knew she was holding something back.

"What is it, Ellen?"

Her friend exhaled a sigh, as though relieved to have been asked. "Look, don't be mad at me, but when you said about him and Tammy, I couldn't help myself. I did a bit of digging into him. I think I know something else about Michael, but I want to make sure my suspicions are correct first."

"What are you talking about? You're not going to confront him are you? Please, don't, Ellen. He's dangerous."

She was terrified Ellen would try to say something to Michael. Ellen might find herself suddenly compelled to throw herself off the side of a cliff, or take an overdose of drugs, or slit her wrists in the bath.

"He's not going to make me hurt myself, Livvy. Tammy was into drugs, and you're ... well ... you."

"What does that mean?"

Ellen squeezed her hand. "I'm only going to talk to him."

"No! Can't you see? That's when he's the most dangerous."

Movement came from the foot of the bed, and a doctor appeared with a number of younger doctors trailing along behind him.

"This is Olivia Midhurst. Twenty-seven years old. She's been admitted with lacerations to her inner wrists. Suspected attempted suicide."

Her cheeks flared hot as numerous sets of eyes regarded her.

"Hi, Olivia," the male doctor said, speaking to her directly now, where he'd only previously been talking to his colleagues. "I'm Dr. Collins. Mind if I take a quick look at you?"

Olivia shook her head and wished the thin mattress of the hospital bed would open up and swallow her.

Ellen released her hand and got up from her seat. "You need to get some rest." She leaned in and gave Liv a quick hug. "I'll come back first thing tomorrow and bring some of your things back in for you."

"Wait, Ellen. What's the other thing? What have you found out about him?"

But Ellen had already turned and walked away, her back vanishing through the doorway.

Shit. Shit, shit, shit.

Tears of anger and frustration filled her eyes. She couldn't let Ellen go and find Michael.

She turned her attention to the doctors. "I really am fine. I don't need all of this. I didn't mean to cause a fuss."

Dr. Collins smiled down at her. "Before we can discharge you, we need to bring someone in to talk to you about what happened. We're stretched thin right now, but we hope to have someone come in by the morning to see how you are."

"How I am? You mean how I am mentally?"

"Yes. Your injuries are only superficial, but considering everything..."

"I need to go. I'm fine, I promise. It was just a cry for help."

He patted her arm. "And that's why we're going to get you some."

"No, please. I need to go. My friend—"

He shook his head, his lips pressed together. "I'm afraid I'm really going to have to insist, Olivia. You know we can always get the police involved if you do try to leave before you speak to someone. You'll be deemed at a risk to yourself."

She snatched her arm away. "Fine, I'll stay."

"Glad to hear it. Now, try to get some rest, and someone will be around to speak with you in the morning."

The doctor and his little group of followers moved on to the next bed, leaving Olivia frozen with impotent fear and anger. She needed to go after Ellen, but if she tried to leave now, the doctors and nurses would call the police and have her sectioned. If she ended up sectioned against her will, she could be in there for weeks, if not months, and Michael would be free to do whatever the hell he wanted.

What had Ellen learned about him? Had she done some online research after Tammy had died? Perhaps something she'd said had sparked Ellen's suspicions, and she'd decided to check him out for herself.

Liv must have been one of the only people in the modern dating world who didn't automatically Google and online stalk the men she was interested in. Perhaps it was because she'd hate the idea of someone doing that to her. She knew if someone Googled her name they'd discover Olivia Midhurst only came into existence a couple of years ago. Now, however, she was wondering if her lack of curiosity had been her downfall. From what Ellen had said, it sounded as though her friend had done a little digging of her own and found out some dirt on Michael. Was Ellen going to confront him now? Did that mean she knew where he lived or had she got his phone number? It wouldn't have been difficult to get. All Ellen would have needed to do was check Olivia's phone and she'd have quickly come across the number. The thought of Ellen confronting Michael terrified her. What if he did the same to her as he done to Tammy and God only knew how many women before her? Depression and suicide were a modern-day epidemic, and a death that looked as though it was done by their own hand wouldn't be questioned.

She needed to get out of here, but she didn't have anything with her. Her bag and phone were left back at the flat when she'd been brought here. She couldn't even call Ellen to make sure she was all right. She needed to sneak out of the hospital, but she couldn't do it right now. There were too many people around. She needed to wait until the night shift started and there were fewer doctors and nurses around. They'd already threatened to call the police if she tried to leave, so she needed to appear as cooperative as possible.

Time passed by frustratingly slowly. Every minute that went by was another minute Ellen might be in danger. Nurses came around to re-bandage and clean her arms. The doctors hadn't used traditional stitches for her wounds, but instead had used a type of tape which held the cuts together. She caught a glimpse of them under her bandage. They weren't as bad as she'd imagined, and they were even less on her right arm. Was that what had saved her life? If she'd managed to cut her right arm as well as the left, would she have died? Why hadn't she gone all the way and slit the wrist of her right hand? Or even cut from her wrist to her elbow instead of across? Had she known, deep down, this was wrong, or had it simply been a practical thing that had saved her life? She remembered the blade getting slippery with blood and how difficult it had been to hold it while she was trying to cut herself. The next thing she remembered was waking up on the floor of her bathroom surrounded by the paramedics and Ellen. Had she passed out from the blood loss, or had she suffered another blackout? Perhaps she should have mentioned the blackouts to the doctors. She was surprised Ellen hadn't said anything herself. Her friend probably hadn't thought of it amid the latest chaos. The blackouts troubled her. She didn't think she could put those down to Michael, even though they had only started once he'd come into her life.

Why was that? Had she subconsciously known she wouldn't be able to handle having Michael in her life, or was there something physically wrong with her, and the events with Michael were just a coincidence?

The ward housekeeper brought her a tray of food—a slop of mess in two separate compartments that she didn't even taste as she was eating. But Liv knew the routine and understood how this worked. If she ate, smiled, nodded, and made eye-contact, the staff would be less worried about her and were less likely to keep watch over her. The ones who were withdrawn and not eating were the ones they'd be watching more closely.

Chapter Twenty-eight
Three Days Earlier

THE HOURS WENT BY, and eventually the shifts swapped over, the day shift going home and leaving a more skeleton crew of the night shift. Lights were dimmed to allow people to sleep, and she knew her time to escape was fast approaching. She only hoped she wasn't too late.

Thankfully, she hadn't been prescribed any kind of sedative, and, other than the throbbing in her left wrist where she'd cut herself the worst, she felt physically all right. They'd given her a hospital gown for when they'd been working on her cuts, but the jeans and t-shirt she'd been wearing when she'd been brought in were packed into a bag beneath the hospital bed. Ellen had promised she'd bring clean clothes and toiletries in for her the following day, but Liv didn't plan on being in hospital long enough for that to happen. Besides, if Ellen went to Michael first, there was a good chance she might not make it to Liv's flat to get her belongings. If she pissed Michael off, there was no telling what he might do.

Liv threw back the white hospital sheet and slipped out of bed. In her bare feet, she padded over to the railing which held the privacy curtain that ran along the rail attached to the ceiling. She knew it was a risk pulling it across, and that it might catch the nurses' attention and make them think she was using the privacy to harm herself, but there didn't look to be anyone around right now, and plenty of the other patients had done the same things to allow them some privacy while they slept.

Liv had no intention of sleeping, however.

Crouching, she pulled the bag containing her clothes out from under her bed. She worked quickly, her pulse racing, as she yanked off the hospital gown and swapped them for her t-shirt and jeans. Her stomach sank as she realised the clothes were covered in her blood. The red stains had dried dark—blotches of blacks and browns—but, together with her bandaged wrists, she looked as though she was dressed up for Halloween. She was bound to get unwanted attention like this.

Unsure what else to do, she picked the discarded gown back up, and pulled it over her clothes. The hem hung low, hiding most of her jeans, and the long sleeves hid her bandaged wrists. But the hospital gown meant she belonged at the hospital, and she was going to get noticed if she wandered out looking like this. She didn't dare put her trainers back on yet in case someone asked her to get out of bed, or pulled back the sheets. The clothes she'd be able to hide or make an excuse for, but she wouldn't be able to explain away wearing shoes.

She pulled back the privacy curtain again and quickly climbed back into bed and pulled the sheets over her legs to hide the bottom of her jeans. Someone would come around to check on her soon, and she wanted to appear as though she was sleeping, and therefore was nothing to be concerned about. If her drawing back the curtain had caught someone's attention, then seeing her peacefully lying in bed should abate any concerns.

Liv warred with her desire to get the hell out of there, and her need to make sure no one noticed her leaving. It felt as though an hour or more had passed, but finally she heard the solid footsteps of sensible footwear as they walked past her bed. Liv froze, tense beneath the sheets, keeping her eyes shut and trying to make her breathing even. She hoped the nurse wouldn't be able to hear the thunder of her heartbeat.

The footsteps stopped, and she heard the flip of paper as they checked her chart hooked on the end of the bed. The person cleared their throat and then kept moving on to check on the next unfortunate soul who'd ended up spending their night here.

She waited long enough to be sure the nurse had left the ward and then risked opening an eye. Everything was still, even if it wasn't silent. People coughed, someone cried quietly, another person muttered in their sleep, while someone else moaned in pain. She didn't think she'd be getting much sleep here even if she wanted to.

With the plan of telling someone she was looking for the bathroom if she was stopped, Liv slipped back out of bed. She still had the hospital gown covering her regular clothes, but she'd need to get rid of it soon.

She bent and pulled on her trainers, keeping her head up to spot if anyone was coming, and then she left the bed and hurried to the door out in the corridor. The nurses' station was at the far end, but if she went in the opposite direction and looped around, she should come out behind them.

A leather jacket had been left slung over the back of a chair just inside one of the other rooms. Without pausing, she scooped it up and kept going. The sign for the toilets was ahead, and she pushed her way through the door. Without even going into the stall, she pulled the hospital gown over her head and then put on the jacket. It was a man's jacket and was too big for her, but it meant it hung down over her bandaged wrists, and when she zipped it up, it hid most of her bloodied clothing. Then she pulled her hair out of the ponytail it had been in and let it float in waves around her face.

Liv stopped to look at herself in the mirror, staring into her own pale eyes.

"You can do this," she told her reflection. "This is for Ellen."

She took a deep breath to steady her nerves then left the bathroom.

This would be the hardest part, walking past the nurses' station and out into the reception area and waiting room for Accident and Emergency. Liv held herself straighter, walking with a confidence she didn't feel. The nurses' station was to her right, and the doors leading into A&E were directly ahead. Liv focused on the door and prayed no one could hear how her heartbeat thundered like horses' hooves.

She reached the doors, and they opened automatically. Forcing herself to remain at a walk instead of breaking into a run, which was what she really wanted to do, she left the ward and stepped out into reception. Beyond the desk, a number of people were still waiting to be seen.

"Hello? Can I help you?" a voice called to her from the reception desk, and set her pulse racing.

Liv lifted her hand in a wave, not bothering to turn and look so they didn't get a look at her face. Her red hair was distinctive, but she hoped having it down made it less recognisable. "Sorry. Took a wrong turn."

Accident and Emergency was busy no matter the time of day, and she was thankful for all the people. She blended in with the drunks, and injuries, but the whole time she was tensed, waiting for the shout that would signal she'd been missed.

The main doors leading to freedom were right ahead of her. Liv could hardly believe she'd managed to get away with it as they slid open in response to her presence and she stepped out into fresh air. An ambulance waited in the bay in front. She put her head down and kept going, shivering from the chill laced on the night air. She didn't have any money to get a taxi, or even have her Oyster card to get the Tube, or her phone to order an Uber. She only had her feet to rely on.

At least she knew her way around London. It would take her a good forty minutes to walk home, possibly longer, but she didn't have any choice. She hoped she was up to it physically. She'd lost blood when she'd cut herself, but otherwise she felt okay.

Liv put her head down and kept going. Would someone have thought to lock the front door of her flat when they left? She hoped in the chaos of the ambulance journey they wouldn't have thought to. She remembered how Ellen said she was going to go back and get some of her things, so she hoped that meant the door was still open, as she didn't have a key, and only Tammy had had the other key. If Ellen had got there before her, she would almost definitely have picked up the keys and locked the front door as well, but if she'd figured she'd go there in the morning, there was the chance the door would still be open. She hoped so. She didn't want to have to break into her own flat. It was bound to get her attention she could do without.

Her body ached by the time she reached Shepherd's Bush. She was exhausted and wanted to sleep, but adrenaline pushed her on. She wouldn't be able to stay here, even if she wanted to. As soon as the hospital noticed her missing and did a search of the premises to find her gone, they would send the police to her known address. She doubted it would be urgent—someone like her wouldn't rank high on their list of priorities—but they'd come eventually.

Liv climbed the stairs of her building—even exhausted and weak from blood loss, she couldn't bring herself to use the lift—and was relieved and cautious to find her door unlocked, though at least either Ellen or the paramedics had thought to pull it shut behind them when they'd left.

"Hello?"

She didn't know who might be here, but this was London, after all. People sneaked into places to steal or squat. After the last few days, all her senses were on high alert, and she had no choice but to be cautious.

The place looked exactly as she'd left it. Ellen hadn't been here yet, and that worried her. Would she have left it until the morning? Maybe, if she had plans to go and find Michael first to confront him.

She braved poking her head into the bathroom. Blood was smeared across the floor and sink, red against the white tiles. Avoiding the worst of the mess, she leaned over to open the medicine cabinet above the sink. The small tub of her medication sat on a shelf. Her mind blurred. When was the last time she'd taken her pills? She'd always been so meticulous, but with everything that had happened, she'd lost track of the time and days, and she couldn't be sure when she'd last taken a dose. She took the pot down and cracked off the lid. She tipped a couple of the pills into her palm. She was only supposed to take one at a time, but perhaps she should take more to make up for the ones she missed.

But what if the pills have been causing the blackouts, a little voice whispered in her head. *They might be making you sicker. Maybe you shouldn't take any at all.*

Liv hesitated, staring down at the pills in the centre of her palm. She dug her teeth into her lower lip, hard enough to hurt, and tasted blood. She wasn't sure how long she stood there for, but eventually she exhaled a sigh and tipped the pills back into the pot. A clear head was vital, and she didn't trust them right now.

Leaving the bathroom, she went back into her bedroom to find her phone. Where had she left it? She checked the bed, and bedside table, and floor. It wasn't here. What about the living room? When had she last had it?

If she couldn't find it to call Ellen, she'd need to go over to Ellen's flat and see if she could find her there. She hoped her friend would be tucked up in bed, or curled up on the sofa watching a film. As long as she hadn't gone to find Michael, she would be safe.

Unless Michael tries to find her ...

With relief, she spotted her mobile phone on the coffee table. "Oh, thank God." She snatched it up and checked the screen. There weren't any missed calls, which meant no one had alerted Ellen that she was missing from the hospital yet.

She scrolled through the phone, found Ellen's number, and hit call. Liv placed it to her ear and waited anxiously as it rang.

"Come on, pick up." She paced across the flat, chewing on the corner of her thumbnail until the area was raw and bleeding. But the call went through to answer phone. "It's me," Liv said. "Call me back. I need to know you're okay."

She hung up and called again, but once more the answer phone kicked in.

"Shit."

She was going to have to go over to Ellen's place.

Liv spotted the keys for the estate agency's car. She'd attached them to the Richmond keys for safekeeping and had forgotten to take them off and sign them back in, she realised with a twinge of guilt. She hoped she wouldn't get in trouble for it at work, but that was probably the least of her worries.

Still, the car meant it would be quicker to reach Ellen's. There was little traffic on the road at this time of the night. All she needed was to know her friend was safe, and she'd be able to handle whatever came after that. She pocketed the keys and phone and turned to the door.

Liv froze, her heart lurching into her throat.

The front door was opening.

Someone was here.

Chapter Twenty-nine
Two Days Earlier

EVERYTHING WAS DARK.

Liv groaned, her whole body aching. The back of her head thudded and her cut arm throbbed. What had happened?

She'd been at her flat; she remembered that much. But after that ...

She sought her memory, trying to figure out the events after, but there was nothing. Had she suffered another blackout? Or had someone attacked her?

Michael.

With a groan, Liv clambered to her feet, ignoring her pounding head and throbbing arm. It was dark, so at first she didn't know where she was. This wasn't her place, though. Where was she? Had Michael brought her back to his home? As her eyes grew used to the dark, she took in her surroundings. She was in a small but comfortable looking living room. There was an L-shaped sofa with a throw and a number of cushions, a thick rug, and a glass coffee table. With a jolt, she realised she knew where she was, and it wasn't Michael's. From the sideboard, a picture inside a frame stared out at her. Ellen and Ryan. She was at Ellen's flat.

Confusion filled her. How had she got here?

Panic surged through her, and she patted down the pockets of the leather jacket she'd stolen. The bulges of keys and her phone were beneath her palms. Snatching the phone out of her pocket, she tried to call Ellen again. Still no answer, and there was no sign of ringing from within the flat.

A heavy stone of dread had lodged in her gut.

There was only one explanation.

Michael.

Michael must have done something to her.

It would have been easy enough for him to find out where Ellen lived. If he'd told her to do something to herself, then she might have taken herself off somewhere to do it. Only he'd know where that was, as Ellen clearly wasn't here. London was a big place.

A certainty and resolution solidified within her. She needed to get Michael somewhere she'd be able to make him talk. She needed to be able to question him. But there was one major flaw in her plan. If he talked, he'd be able to make her do things she didn't want to do.

Something else wasn't quite adding up. If Michael was responsible for getting her to Ellen's, then where was he now? Why had he just brought her here and dumped her?

Curious, Liv went to the window and pulled back the blind. The agency car was parked outside on the street.

Fuck. She must have driven herself. Had she suffered another blackout? Her mind was spinning. She couldn't think about it, the dizziness only getting worse the more she tried to concentrate and remember what had happened. She pulled her thoughts away, frightened she'd black out again. Did that mean

Michael hadn't been the one to bring her here—she'd come here by herself, looking for Ellen, perhaps?

There was only one thing left she could do.

She redialled the phone, this time calling Michael.

"Stop calling me, Olivia."

The sound of his voice made her skin crawl. "Where's Ellen?" she demanded.

"I have no idea."

"Don't lie to me!"

"I'm not."

She could tell he was speaking through gritted teeth.

"I know your dirty little secret," she bluffed. "You might think you've kept Ellen's mouth shut, and that you'd dealt with me. Well, this is your wake-up call. I know all about you. Ellen told me everything. Meet me at this address in an hour, or I'll make sure everyone else knows as well."

She hung up and then quickly texted him the address. She needed to move to make sure she got there before he did, if he even showed.

Yes, he'd show. She knew him well enough to know that much, at least.

She left Ellen's flat, pulling the door shut behind her, and ran to the car. She was breathing hard, her palms sweaty, her body aching. Adrenaline pumped through her veins. The car door was open, so she clearly hadn't bothered to lock it when she'd arrived, but then she was amazed she'd even managed to drive, considering she couldn't remember a single part of the journey. Sliding into the driver's seat, she jammed the keys in the ignition and brought the car to life.

Liv put her foot down, thankful for the lack of traffic. It was a twenty-minute drive, and she needed to get there before Michael. Her mind was in a spin and she struggled to think straight. She needed to if she was going to beat him, however. She drove past a twenty-four hour supermarket and suddenly swerved. Though she needed to get to the property, an idea had started to form in her mind, and she was going to need supplies to see it through.

She was aware of how she looked. Her jeans were stained dark with blood, but the leather jacket covered the worst of the stains on her top. She didn't have any money with her, but she had a paying app on her phone, so she was able to use that. The supermarket catered for everything, and she whipped around, finding the items she needed, including a cheap rucksack to shove it all into. The young man working the till moved frustratingly slowly, and it was all she could do to stop herself from yelling at him to hurry things up. She needed to remember the hospital may well have called the police by now if they thought she was a danger to herself or others, and anything that would make her more memorable would be a bad thing.

Finally, she was able to scan her phone to pay and grab the things she'd bought. She hurried back out to the car and climbed behind the wheel. She was banking on Michael having been at home when she called, so he would have much further to come than she did, giving her the extra time. This would get a lot harder if he reached the place before her.

Within fifteen minutes, she pulled up outside the property and hit the button on the fob to open the gates. A sigh of relief escaped her lungs as she noted Michael hadn't arrived yet. She'd need to move the car, and his car, too, when he did, but for the moment, she just needed to get him inside the house.

Liv climbed out and pulled the bag of gear out with her.

Damn. She should have thought to bring a weapon of some kind. It wasn't as though she could have bought something in the supermarket, though. What she'd purchased was already bad enough without adding a knife or something similar to the haul. Raising people's suspicions, especially when the police might already be on the lookout for her because of her escape from the hospital, was the last thing she wanted to do.

Standing in the driveway, she looked around, hoping to spot something, though she had no idea what. Her gaze alighted on a flowerbed and the canes sticking out of the dirt that had been support for some long dead flowers in the garden. It wasn't much, but she was running out of time. With the bag clutched in her other hand, she ran over and pulled one of the canes out of the ground. Experimentally, she swept the cane through the air.

It wasn't exactly a knife or a gun, but it could certainly do some damage. She didn't want Michael dead; she just wanted to get Ellen's location out of him.

She had the keys to the property on the car keys, so she fumbled what she was holding for a moment and managed to get the front door open. The property was exactly as she remembered it—a wide open entrance hall with the chequered flooring. And there, beneath the stairs, was the door that led down to the cellar.

The cellar had given her the creeps last time she was here, but now she was going to have to force herself to spend time down there, and with the person she feared most in the world.

Had being spooked by the place come from some subconscious understanding of what the future held for her? There was no need to be frightened of things that went bump in the dark when real life held far greater terrors.

She opened the cellar door and flicked on the switch for the light, her fingers finding it easily this time. Stepping through the door, Liv paused at the top of the stairs. She was looking at this place from a different perspective this time, checking for weak spots he might be able to use against her. She spotted something she hadn't the first time—a bolt on the back of the door. She narrowed her eyes. What would the owners have used that for? Why would they have wanted to keep people out of here? What had they been doing? Her gaze went back to the hook embedded in the low ceiling. She'd assumed it had been used to hang game or some other kind of meat, perhaps something that would have gone well with the expensive wine they'd most likely have kept down here—but now she wondered if it had been used for something else entirely.

Not wanting to waste any more time, Liv hurried down the stairs and paused beneath the hook. She dropped the bag from her shoulder and stooped down, tugging open the top and pulling out what she needed. Rope and a length of material she'd use as a gag. She unravelled the rope and stood on tiptoes to loop one end over the hook and tied it tight. Was she doing the right thing, or should she wait and tie his hands first, assuming it even got this far? She didn't know. It wasn't as though she'd ever done this before.

Suddenly panicked that he might have already arrived and would catch her down here preparing, she left both the bag and the cane where they were and turned and ran back up the stairs.

She'd left the front door open, and when she peered through, the driveway was still in darkness. He hadn't yet arrived.

Steeling her nerves, she went on the hunt for the next thing she needed.

The property wasn't furnished, but there were still a few items left inside. She remembered seeing something she could use beside the huge marble fireplace. Leaving the cellar for the moment, she hurried into the living room. Beside the wood burner was an iron fireside tool set. She hurried over and picked up the poker. The metal was cool in her palm, the weight of the item surprisingly heavy. The cane wouldn't be any use initially, when she first needed to take him down, but this would do.

Outside, headlights swept down the road in front of the house, followed by the sound of an engine. The engine cut out, but the headlights continued to illuminate the street.

Liv's pulse jack-knifed, every muscle in her body taut with anticipation. It was him. She was sure. She needed to act quickly. If she gave him the chance to speak, he would be able to control her actions and influence how she acted next, and then she'd never find out where Ellen was.

She tightened her fingers around the handle of the poker and went to the open front door. Positioning herself so the poker was on the other side of the doorframe, hiding it from view, Liv waited.

The headlights went dark, and a moment later the slam of a car door shutting made her jump. Her heart raced and she felt dizzy with tension, but there was no going back. She needed to keep her nerve.

Michael's tall figure appeared in the open driveway, his feet crunching on gravel. She had the light on behind her, so he probably only saw her silhouette, but she knew he'd recognise her as immediately as she recognised him.

He stopped just inside the open gate. "Olivia. What the fuck is this all about?"

"You need to come with me. I've got something to show you."

"I don't need to do anything you say," he spat.

She couldn't let him talk for long. He might tell her to do something to hurt herself again. "Yes, you do. At least, you do if you don't want everyone to know your dirty little secret."

With that, she turned, keeping the poker close to her body so he wouldn't see it, and walked deeper into the house.

"What the hell, Olivia?" he called after her.

But she didn't respond. She imagined his frustration, hesitating as he decided what to do. Should he go back to his car and risk her spilling whatever Ellen had found out about him, or should he go after her and try to minimise the damage?

The crunch of footsteps signalled him walking towards the house, and Liv caught her breath and ducked back in against the wall. He wouldn't be able to see her now, and she was able to move back towards the front door, staying hidden from sight.

The footsteps grew closer, and then went quiet as his feet left the gravel and hit the paving slabs which led up to the front door.

With trembling arms, Liv took the poker in both hands and lifted it above her head.

"Olivia?" He stepped through the front door.

And Liv brought the poker down, the metal cracking against his skull.

Chapter Thirty
Present Day

"NO!"

Her scream cut through the air.

His hand was free now, and she knew exactly what he was going to do next. He'd reach for the gag and pull it away from his mouth, and then he'd make her do whatever he wanted.

Still, she didn't give in. Even though deep down she thought all hope was lost, she scrambled to her feet and threw herself at him. He still had one hand tied to the metal hook in the ceiling, but, just as she'd thought he would, instead of trying to untie that hand using the one he'd freed, his fingers went straight to the gag at his mouth.

His words were his weapon.

She caught his freed arm, dragging it away from his face, but he shook her off. She was injured, and even with him half tied up, he was stronger than she was. Everything hurt. Her face throbbed, and the back of her head pulsed with pain. She was tired, so tired, and she just wanted all of this to be over.

His fingers hooked the gag and he yanked it from his mouth. "Stop it, Olivia. For fuck's sake. Just stop."

It was done. Micheal was free. Now she'd die, too.

Liv dropped to her knees, giving in to great, painful sobs. She put her hands over her face and cried until the salty tears mixed with the blood, and the combination dripped through her fingers and onto her jean-covered thighs.

"What are you going to make me do?" she cried.

He stared at her with those deep brown eyes—eyes she'd once convinced herself she'd cared for. "Make you do? I can't make you do anything."

His hand was working the knots that bound his other wrist to the metal hook now. He'd be free soon. Not that it mattered. It was all over.

"I know what you can do," she said, lifting her eyes to his, forcing herself to be brave even though she knew she wouldn't have much longer to live. "I know you hurt those women."

"What the fuck are you talking about, Liv? I haven't hurt anyone."

"Okay, maybe you didn't physically hurt them, but you made them hurt themselves."

Confusion clouded his features. "How the hell did I do that?"

She staggered back to her feet. "Don't lie to me! I don't know how you do it, but you're able to make people do things. You tell them to do it, and it puts the thought into their head. You've done it with me plenty of times, and you did it to the others as well."

"I seriously have no fucking idea what you're talking about."

She shook her head and pointed her finger at him. "This! This is what you do. You twist people's way of thinking. I don't know how you do it, but you do. That's how you got Holly Newie to kill herself."

The confusion didn't leave his face. "Who the fuck is Holly Newie?"

"The blonde woman I caught you fighting with that day near Hyde Park. The one who went missing and then killed herself. Don't make out like you didn't have anything to do with it."

"I didn't!" he protested.

"And then Tammy? You were the last person to speak to her. You'd fought with her about me, and then she showed up dead."

"It was a drug overdose, Liv."

"No!" She jabbed her finger at him again. "That's just what you wanted everyone to think. You told her to O.D., I know you did. It was your way of getting her out of your life."

"You're insane. Yes, I argued with Tammy, but only because I thought she was a total bitch towards you. There's no possible way I could have got her to overdose. Tammy was a party girl. She was doing class A drugs every weekend. It was only a matter of time."

She shook her head. "No, I don't believe you. How do you explain Ellen going missing as well, then? I know she found out something about you. She was going to speak to you, and I begged her not to because I knew how dangerous you are. Then she just goes missing! You think that's a coincidence?"

"No, I don't think it's a coincidence," he said coolly.

She jumped on the admission. "So, you're saying you did do something to them all! Where's Ellen? What did you tell her to do? Is she going to kill herself, too?"

"Shut up, Olivia."

Her mouth snapped closed at his tone.

"It isn't a coincidence," he continued, "because you're also the person who links all these women together."

"What the hell are you talking about? They're my friends."

He shook his head. "You're wrong. Ellen might have been, but not the others. You didn't even know the blonde woman, but you were immediately suspicious and jealous about me talking to her, and deep down you hated Tammy."

She shook her head again. "You're lying. You hurt Ellen, or you've told her to go somewhere and kill herself, just like you did the others!"

"You're the one who's done this, Olivia. It's more likely that you're the one who killed that blonde woman you saw me speaking to, and you probably killed Tammy. I don't know where Ellen is because I bet you're the one who took her. God only knows what you did to her. You've probably killed her, too."

Tears streamed down her face. "No, no, no, no ..." It wasn't true. It couldn't be true. Yet she'd been missing chunks of time. Was that when it had happened? Had she killed Tammy, blaming the other woman for trying to take Michael away from her? Had she killed Ellen, too? "No, you're trying to put thoughts in my head again. You're trying to make me believe things that aren't true. That's what you do. You make people do bad things!"

"You're insane. Do you actually believe that? I'm not the bad one here, Olivia. That's you. You've kept me here, tortured me to get information from me, when all this time, the only one with that information is you. I don't know where Ellen is, but I think you do. I bet you're the one who took her, and it wouldn't surprise me if she's dead, too!"

"No! She was coming to find you. You're the link here. You're the one who made them hurt themselves. Just like you made me hurt myself, too."

"You crazy bitch. Ellen came to me. She found out something about me, and warned me off of you. The poor woman didn't want to see you get hurt, which is laughable in itself, considering you were the one doing the hurting this whole time anyway."

"What do you mean, she didn't want me to get hurt? Had she figured out what you're able to do?"

"No! Stop it with that bullshit. I can't do anything. That is all in your head. Ellen came to talk to me because she found out I was married."

She stared at him. "Married?"

"Yeah, I have a wife and a three-year-old son, too. That's why I never let you come back to my house, and why I wasn't around some weekends. They're probably worried sick right now, wondering what's happened to me. I might have been away for 'work' on occasions, but I've almost always answered my phone. I expect they've called the police by now to report me missing. They'll be out looking for me."

She shook her head, frantic. "No, there's more to it than that. You're able to do something. You can make people do what you want them to do. You make people hurt themselves. They do something to upset you, and you tell them to go kill themselves!"

"Like I did with you, you mean?"

"Exactly!" She rolled up her sleeves to show him her bandaged wrists.

"Olivia, you hurt yourself because you wanted to. Because you know you're fucked up in the head and you were hurting people. Yeah, I said it, but I didn't make you do it."

"Yes, you did. It's some kind of dangerous mind control. Or hypnotism. Or something."

"You're so far off the mark, this would be funny if you weren't so fucking dangerous. What were you really taking those tablets for—what were they? Anti-psychotics. Don't tell me they were for a bit of anxiety. It was worse than that, wasn't it? That guy in the street that day, the one who called you Sarah, he actually did know you, didn't he?"

She clutched her hands to her ears, not wanting to hear him say another word. "Stop it, stop it."

"Sarah? Is that your real name? Sarah."

She battered at her head with her hands. "Stop it," she shrieked, "stop it!"

"I'm innocent. You've been torturing an innocent man all this time."

"You're not innocent. You were married and sleeping with me!"

"Maybe, but you're the one who is dangerous. You're the only one who knows where Ellen is, or what happened to the other women."

"That's not true." But was it? Her mind flickered, trying to rearrange her reality. No, she didn't want to know. Didn't want to remember.

"What did you do to, Ellen, Sarah?" Michael said, using her real name. "What did you do to your best friend?"

Chapter Thirty-one
Three Days Earlier

THE FRONT DOOR OF LIV'S flat opened.

Someone was here.

The keys for the agency car were tight in her fist, her phone in the other hand. She'd been trying to call Ellen, but it had just gone straight to answer phone. Now someone was here, and there was only one person she thought it would be.

Michael.

He had done something to Ellen, and now he was here to mess with her, too.

But to her surprise, a familiar blonde, curvy figure stepped through the door. She was looking down, so didn't notice Liv standing there until Liv spoke.

"Ellen?"

Her friend looked up in shock. "Liv? What the hell are you doing here? You're supposed to be in hospital. I was just stopping by to get your things for the morning."

"Why didn't you answer your phone? I've been calling you. I've been worried sick."

"The battery died." Her tone grew firm. "Why aren't you in hospital, Liv?"

"I left. I had to. I needed to know you were going to be all right. Did you see Michael?"

Ellen nodded. "Yes, I did. I've warned him to stay away from you."

"Oh, my God, Ellen. I told you not to go near him. He's dangerous."

She shook her head, her eyebrows drawn together, her nose wrinkled. "He's not going to come sniffing around again, Liv. I promise. I've threatened him—"

"Threatened him? Threatened him with what?"

"You don't need to know that. Just know that he won't come near you again. He's not been good for you, Liv."

She didn't care about herself. She caught Ellen by the shoulders. "What did he say to you? Did he tell you to hurt yourself?"

Her face creased in a frown. "Not this again. Michael can't make someone do something just by telling them to."

"He might have made you forget. Or maybe he hasn't done it yet. But you're in danger, Elles, I know you are."

"I'm fine, Livvy. Please. You're not well. I really think you should go back to hospital. The doctors can take care of you there."

She shook her head, frantic. "No, I can't go back there. If I'm back there, who's going to make sure you're all right? If you threatened Michael, he's going to want to get rid of you. Even if he didn't say something when you saw him, I promise you that he'll have something planned. It's what he does with every woman who upsets him."

Ellen shook her head and took a tentative step backwards. "You need help. This is crazy. Go to the police if you think Michael is dangerous."

"I can't. They'll never believe me. I'll be the one who ends up locked up, and he'll be free to do whatever the hell he wants. You'll be next, Ellen. I know you will."

"I'm fine, Liv, I promise. He can't hurt me."

But Liv wasn't buying it. If he knew Ellen had something over him, he wouldn't just let it go.

"I need to show you something," she told her friend.

Ellen's lips twisted, but she nodded and followed Liv as she turned and went back into her bedroom. She went to the adjoining bathroom, a plan starting to formulate in her mind. She felt horrible for doing it, but she didn't have any choice. She needed to keep Ellen safe—that was the most important thing of all.

"I've been on medication," she said as she went into the tiny en-suite bathroom that was off her bedroom. She opened the door to the medicine cabinet and took down her pot of antipsychotics, and another pot, too. "They keep me level, or at least are supposed to, but I don't think they've been working too well lately."

Ellen was standing behind her, and she clung onto what Liv had said. "That's why you need to go back to the hospital. The doctors can help you there."

Liv cracked open the second pot of pills and emptied a few out into her palm. They were tiny tablets and easy to swallow. She turned, and not giving her friend time to question what she was doing, lunged for Ellen.

Ellen hadn't been prepared at all. Liv was so much taller than she was, and Ellen fell backwards, her head smacking on the floor. She was dazed, Liv could see by the way her eyes rolled, but she couldn't give her friend time to come around. Though she felt awful doing it, she pressed her thumb and fingers either side of Ellen's cheeks and forced her mouth open. Ellen must have half realised what was happening, as she tried to twist her face away, but Liv was bigger and stronger. She pried open her friend's lips and dropped the tablets down the back of her throat. Then she clamped her hand over Ellen's mouth to prevent her spitting them back out or shouting for help.

"I'm sorry," she said, still pinning her down. "It's just something that will help you sleep. This is for your own safety. I promise. I need to make sure he can't find you."

Ellen's eyes widened and she shook her head beneath Liv's palm. She tried to speak, but her words were muffled. She struggled against Liv's hold, kicking her legs and trying to lift her arms to claw at Liv's face, but Olivia used her entire body weight to pin her down, and any scratches she delivered fell harmlessly against the leather jacket Liv had stolen.

Liv felt wretched. She didn't want her friend to be frightened, but what choice did she have? She would rather Ellen was frightened for a short while than dead for good. Ellen struggled, but as the drugs worked their way into her system, she gradually grew weaker, until she finally fell still.

"I'm sorry," Liv said again, but she was asleep now and couldn't hear her.

Liv looked around for her next step. Her gaze landed on a small walk-in wardrobe. That would do.

She climbed off her friend and caught hold of her ankles. With her back bent and straining, she dragged Ellen into the wardrobe. She didn't want to tie her up, not wanting to leave her defenceless if Michael somehow found her before Liv found him. She wouldn't keep her here for long, she hoped, but Ellen would need to remain here for as long as she was in danger. Thinking of something else, she remembered Ellen's bag. Ellen had dropped it when Liv had jumped her, but a quick rummage through located the keys to Ellen's flat. Ellen might need a change of clothes or something, so at least now Liv had the keys and was able to let herself in when needed.

There was one more problem, however. She needed to figure out how to keep Ellen in the wardrobe. She'd just let herself out again when she woke.

If she found some wood, she'd be able to hammer the doors shut.

There was a skip out the back of the block of flats—Liv had noticed it a couple of times. There was bound to be some discarded wooden planks or boards there she could use, and they had nails and a hammer in the flat from all the times they'd needed to put up pictures or shelves.

Yes, she'd barricade Ellen in with the wooden planks, and let her out as soon as she knew her friend would be safe.

Chapter Thirty-two
Present Day

SHE STAGGERED BACK from Michael. "No. Oh, no."

Liv covered her face with her hands as the memories flooded over her. She'd blacked out because she hadn't wanted to remember what she'd done to Ellen, some part of her knowing that remembering would also mean admitting what she'd been ignoring for so long.

She was sick again.

"You remember, don't you?" Michael demanded. "You know what you did!"

"Ellen. I have to get to Ellen."

"Wait, you fucking bitch! Untie me."

But she ignored him, backing away slowly on shaking legs, before turning and running. Her heart pounded hard in her chest, making her dizzy. She had to hold it together. How long had it been since she'd taken Ellen? Two days? Two days without food or water? Or had she left her something? Her memory was blurry, like pieces of it had been cut away. The medication. She'd stopped taking her meds, had convinced herself they were somehow harming her.

It had happened again, and she hadn't even realised.

Memories of when she'd been Sarah poured back into her mind. A floodgate had been opened. Twenty years old and at university, struggling to hand in coursework and finding exams overwhelming. Had it started then? No, she could go back further, to when she'd been a teen. Her obsessive behaviour, the depression, the self-harm. Her parents had thought she wouldn't cope with the stress of university, but the doctor had put her on anti-depressants, and she'd convinced them she'd be all right.

She hadn't been.

After it had all happened, she went to a psychiatric unit, but then moved back home. She *had* been better, her meds controlling her anxiety and paranoia. But she'd carried the knowledge of what she'd done with her at all times, and she knew she needed to start again. She'd told her parents she was going travelling to stop them looking for her, but then moved to London and changed her name. She sent the occasional email to her parents as Sarah, but told them it was better for her this way, and felt too much contact, or her going back home and seeing them would only make her go backwards in her recovery. Her parents were too nervous of her to argue. She knew they felt like they were constantly walking a tightrope with her, terrified of doing or saying something that might push her over the edge.

So, she'd moved to London and become Olivia Midhurst and had left Sarah Longdown far behind. Or at least she thought she had. Now, it seemed, Sarah had caught up to her once more.

She stumbled up the stairs to the bolted door of the converted wine cellar of the property the estate agency had on its books. The huge, six-bedroom house with its gated driveway and high walls had seemed like the perfect place to take someone if you wanted to get answers out of them. There were no neighbours attached—which was rare in London—and she'd known the place was standing empty. They weren't supposed to be showing anyone around yet, so she hadn't been expecting anyone else to come here. She wondered who had let themselves into the property. One of her colleagues, she expected. How was she going to explain all of this to them? But then she figured her job was going to be the least of her concerns. It wasn't as though she could show people around houses from prison.

She reached the top of the stairs and pulled back the lock with a crack.

"You can't just leave me here, Olivia, or Sarah, or whatever the fuck your name is!" Michael yelled after her. "At least untie me first. After everything you've done, you owe me. You fucking owe me!"

Standing at the top of the stairs, she spun to face him. "You fucking bastard. Don't make out like you're some innocent. I knew something was off about you. Maybe my head twisted everything, but that doesn't mean you're blameless."

Rage contorted his features. "Let me go, you bitch!"

She didn't blame him for his fury, but her head was spinning. She couldn't release him. She wouldn't blame him if he attacked her for what she'd done. She deserved it. But she also remembered what she'd done to Ellen, and her fear for her friend's safety far outweighed any remorse she felt about what she'd put Michael through. Maybe he wasn't guilty of what she'd accused him of, but he'd still been cheating on his wife for the past month, and had lied to them all. It wasn't as though he was a good man.

"I'm sorry," she shouted back at him as she turned for the door. "I'll send the police. They can come and get you, and you can tell them everything. Of course, then I'm sure your wife will also find out everything, but I think that's probably the one good thing that will come out of all of this."

"Fuck! Fuck you, you fucking bitch!"

She ignored him. Hopefully, the last piece of rope would hold long enough to let her get away.

As she ran from the house, memories tumbled over her, coming thicker and faster. Those days leading up to this moment, when she'd truly believed Michael was a danger to both her and everyone around her. She'd only wanted to keep Ellen safe, and when Ellen had told her she'd found something out about Michael and was going to confront him, all she'd wanted to do was keep Ellen safe. So, she'd done what she had, but then her dysfunctional, misfiring, crazy brain had blocked out what she'd done, so all she'd known was that Ellen was missing and Michael was dangerous, and that he was the only one who'd known where she was.

She burst out of the house into fresh air. It was the first she'd tasted in two days, and it hit her lungs like a bucket of cold water. She suddenly became aware of the state she was in. The bandages around her arms which had been administered by the hospital had grown hard and were stinking. All the violence had opened her wounds time and time again, bleeding fresh into the old bandages before crusting over again. She'd be lucky if she didn't get an infection. She still wore those same clothes as well, the bloodied t-shirt and jeans, and the leather jacket she'd stolen. The stink of rot was oozing off her, but she didn't have time to take care of herself. She needed to get to Ellen.

God, she couldn't believe what she had done. She'd forced sleeping tablets down her friend's throat and held her down until she'd passed out. Tears filled Liv's eyes, and she swiped them away, angry at herself. Ellen must have been so confused, so frightened as to why her best friend had suddenly turned on her.

Liv reached the driveway and stood still, looking around. The car wasn't parked here. What had she done with it? Her mind was spinning, all the pieces of what had happened falling into place. She'd taken the agency car. What would Tony have thought when neither she nor Ellen turned up to work? Did he think they'd stolen the vehicle and run off together?

That didn't matter now. What mattered was remembering where she'd left the vehicle.

It came back to her with a jolt, and she snatched a breath before running around the side of the house. There was a double garage attached to the house, and she'd moved the vehicles—both the agency's and Michael's—so they wouldn't be seen. She still had the keys in her pocket, so she opened the garage door to reveal both cars.

With tears streaming down her face, Liv climbed behind the wheel, shoved the car into gear, and stamped down on the accelerator. Her only thought was to reach Ellen. She didn't even care if she was pulled over by the police for speeding—at least then she'd be able to confess what she'd done, and they would go and help her friend.

She drove faster than she'd ever dared to before, and within fifteen minutes she was back at her building. Abandoning the car on double yellow lines outside, she sprinted up the stairs to her flat.

Liv slammed her palms against her front door, astonished that she'd managed to lock her flat on top of everything else. Scrabbling back in the pocket of her stolen jacket, she found the keys and opened the door.

"Ellen!" she cried. "Oh, my God. Ellen, I'm so sorry. I'm coming!"

She burst into her bedroom and gasped as she saw the boards she'd nailed across the doors of her walk in wardrobe. How had she done all this and then completely blocked it from her mind?

"Ellen?" she yelled again. "I'm coming!"

She listened hard for any response, but there wasn't one. *Oh, God, please don't let her be dead. Please don't let her be dead.* She'd never prayed before, not really, but her prayers weren't for her. They were for Ellen, who never deserved any of this.

She yanked off the boards she'd nailed across the doors, splintering her nails but not caring. She lifted her foot, bringing her heel down on the board at the bottom.

"Ellen?" she cried. "Ellen, can you hear me? I'm sorry! I'm so, so sorry!"

But her apologies wouldn't mean a thing if Ellen was dead.

Chapter Thirty-three
Present Day

Olivia yanked away the final board holding her walk-in wardrobe doors together and threw open the door.

"Oh, God."

She reared away as the stench hit her like a slap in the face. This was far worse than the vomit had been back in the wine cellar. This was shit, and piss, and puke. She just prayed it wasn't also the stink of a decomposing body.

It was dark inside the wardrobe, but on the floor she could make out the shape of her friend.

"Ellen!" Tears filled her eyes. She'd done this. She'd done it to her friend. Michael had been right all along. He hadn't been the dangerous one. That had been her. She drugged her friend and then boarded her up inside the wardrobe. What the hell had she been thinking? She hadn't. This wasn't her in her normal state. She'd had a psychotic break again; she knew that now. All the signs had been there, but she'd projected them onto someone else.

The stench was unbearable. Ellen must have used the corner of the wardrobe as a toilet, though Liv could hardly blame her.

Clothes had been pulled from the hangers and used to create a bundle on the floor to sleep on. Cast to one side were metal clothes hangers, bent out of shape. Ellen must have pushed them between the gaps in the door and tried to force off the boards Olivia had nailed on. The metal had been too bendy, however, and the hangers had just changed shape rather than done anything productive. The idea of Ellen, weakened from the drugs, dehydrated, starving, and all the while wondering why her friend had turned on her in such a hideous way. It broke her heart.

She dropped to her knees beside Ellen's body.

"Ellen?" With a trembling hand, she reached out and tentatively rolled Ellen onto her back.

Ellen let out a groan, and Liv clamped her hand over her mouth, holding back a scream.

She was alive.

Realising Ellen had been without water, she scrambled back to her feet and ran into the bedroom. A half drunk, plastic bottle of water was beside the bed, and she snatched it up and took it back to her friend.

"Here," she said, unscrewing the lid and holding it to the other woman's lips. "I brought you some water."

Only barely conscious, Ellen's eyes flickered open. Understanding brightened their blue depths, and they widened as she realised who had shaken her awake.

"No, no, not you!" she croaked.

Ellen managed to get herself onto her elbows, pushing back with her feet.

"It's okay. I'm not going to hurt you. I've come to get you out. I'm so sorry."

Ellen lifted her hands in front of her body to ward her away. "No, I don't believe you. You're crazy. Stay the fuck away from me."

She had been backing away, but now her line of sight landed on the open door behind Olivia, and the freedom it offered. She shot Olivia a wild glance, and Liv was horrified to see how much she'd deteriorated in a matter of days. Her eyes were bruised hollows, her skin waxy and white. Already, the weight loss was visible in the hollows of her cheeks.

"It's okay. You can go. I'm just so relieved to see you're still alive. I was so scared—" Her voice broke, and she pressed her knuckles to her mouth to try and hold it in. "I was so scared you might be dead."

The desperation to run morphed into furious disbelief. "You were scared I might be dead?" Ellen spat. "You did this to me, Olivia! You drugged me and locked me up for days. Don't you dare fucking cry! You don't get to turn on the waterworks for this."

"I'm sorry, I'm sorry. I'm sick. I didn't mean to. I was only trying to keep you safe."

"Well, you could have killed me instead. You need help. Serious help."

Liv nodded. "I know, I know. Please. I brought you some water."

She held the bottle out to Ellen, who hesitated, before reaching out and snatching it from Liv's hand like a stray dog grabbing a snack from a passing stranger. She put the bottle to her lips and drained the contents, before wiping her mouth with the back of her hand.

"This isn't the first time you've got sick like this, is it?" Ellen asked.

She shook her head. "I thought I was better. That's why I moved to London. I wanted to leave it all behind me."

"Leave all what behind you?" Ellen demanded. "What did you do, Olivia?"

Chapter Thirty-four
Seven Years Earlier

DUE TO HER ANXIETY, Sarah Longdown started university late.

She moved into the student halls and tried to forget the reason she was several years older than all the other girls here. She caught them giving her strange glances, as though they could already tell she was the odd one out. On moving in day, the other girls had somehow instantly bonded, though none of them had met each other before, and she was standing on the outskirts looking in. She wished she could understand this somehow easy congeniality other women had with each other. For her, the moment anyone tried to talk to her, she flushed bright red and looked down at her feet, stumbling over her words.

But she'd convinced her parents it was time for her to do this. She was an adult now, twenty years old, and she needed to have a life of her own. She was smart and had done well at school and her exams, despite everything else, and now she felt like she was ready to take the next step.

Besides, student halls was practically like being at home. Or at least it was a good halfway house to having a place of her own. They had security here, so she had someone she could call if anything was bothering her. She'd made a promise to herself that she wasn't going to allow every little thing to spook her, however. The last thing the security guard needed was her calling every few hours because she worried all the time.

Still, those first few days were hard, with everyone seeming to make friends so easily, and her always feeling on the outside. The university did their best to try to encourage everyone to mingle, including a ton of events in the first week of Freshers.

It was at one of the Fresher socials that she first met May. The university social club was at its worst and finest at this time of year, when everyone was putting on a show and many were experiencing freedom for the first time in their lives. It wasn't really her thing, but she hadn't wanted to stay in her room—her need for inclusion warring with her desire to hide away. She'd bought herself a drink, though she knew she couldn't have many or they'd interfere with her meds, and then found herself a corner where she could sit down and watch everyone else dance to a DJ she'd never heard of but who apparently used to play on Radio One.

A second glass slammed down on the table in front of her. "You look like you could use this."

She looked up to see a pretty blonde with thick black-rimmed glasses that she somehow managed to make appear cool and funky standing in front of her. She glanced down at the drink and then back up at the girl, unsure if she'd meant the drink to be for someone else.

"Go on," the blonde said, nudging the drink closer. "It's for you."

"Oh, that's okay. I've already got a drink." She was flustered, her cheeks heating. Attention from anyone—male or female—always caused this reaction in her, and her red hair and pale skin always made the blushing worse.

"Yeah, I know. But if we got to suffer this bunch of dickheads, I figured we'd need some more alcohol." She slid into the seat beside her. "I'm May, by the way."

She surprised a smile out of her. "I'm Sarah."

The blonde, May, stuck out her hand. "It's good to meet you, Sarah. You look like the only sane person in here."

Sarah laughed. The girl couldn't be further from the truth, but she wasn't going to tell her that.

May leaned in closer. "Is it just me, or does everyone here look like they literally left home yesterday."

"I think that's because they did leave home yesterday."

"Losers. I left home when I was seventeen. I couldn't wait to be out of there."

She piqued Sarah's curiosity. "Yeah? How old are you now?"

"Nineteen now, though I'll be twenty in three weeks. How about you?"

"Already twenty," she said, her shoulders sagging in relief. It might have been only a matter of a year or two, but she was relieved to find someone who was basically the same age. All these eighteen-year-olds were driving her crazy.

May laughed. "So, we're the old gits in here, huh?"

"Looks like it."

She lifted her glass and clinked it to Sarah's. "Well, I'll drink to that."

FOR THE NEXT FEW WEEKS, Sarah finally started to feel as though she fit in. May was easy to talk to, and it seemed others felt the same way. May acted like a bridge between Sarah and the other students, and gradually Sarah found herself pulled into the different social groups. May didn't seem to have one group in particular, but lurked on the outskirts of many, yet somehow didn't seem to have the same crippling anxiety Sarah had when it came to going up and speaking to people. They joined a couple of clubs together and got to know people that way, too. But deep down Sarah always knew the new friends were May's friends, really. They tolerated her because May brought her along, but that was all.

Sarah didn't care. Life was easier with May around. They didn't share many classes—May was studying drama, while Sarah was doing English Literature—but it didn't matter. May had a room down the hall from her own, so she was always around when Sarah needed her.

Things were good for awhile. Sarah had finally found her place in the world. Her parents were happy she was doing so well, and it was agreed all round that going to university had been the right decision.

Then May met someone.

Zach was an older guy, in his third year studying marine biology. He and May hit it off right away. He was one of those easy-going, cool guys, who loved to travel and had big dreams of all the exciting places his degree was going to take him. May was besotted, but Sarah could see he wasn't right for her. May followed him around, desperate for even a crumb of his attention. He treated her as though she was only a bit of fun, happy to have around at the weekends, or at a party, but never wanting anything more than that. Sarah tried to get May to understand, but the more she spoke badly of Zach, the more May distanced herself from Sarah. She even tried to warn Zach off a couple of times, telling him that May deserved better than him, but that got back to May, and the two of them fought.

Sarah could feel the distance growing between them, pulling them apart with every passing day. She did everything she could to try to bring them back together again, but the more she tried, the worse it got.

Thoughts started to creep into Sarah's head that something bad would happen to May when they weren't together. At first it was all about Zach, her worrying he would only end up hurting May, but then other things started to creep in. Sarah worried May would be run over by a car, or electrocuted by a rogue plug socket. And then her fears and paranoia, all the little voices whispering in her head about all the bad things that would happen to her, often describing them and the aftermath in detail, started to move outside of her head. She heard the television telling her these things, even when the TV was off, or the radio whispering them into her ear. Then, one night when she was lying in bed, listening to the voices, she realised something. The voices weren't coming from all those other places. No, they were inside the walls of the building.

It wasn't her imagination. Whoever the voices belonged to lived inside the walls, and they were going to hurt May.

Chapter Thirty-five
Present Day

ELLEN STARED AT HER with wide, terrified eyes. "What did you do?" she repeated, still huddled in the nest of Olivia's clothing which she'd created for herself.

Olivia glanced away, her eyes flooding with tears, everything around her shimmering like looking through fractured glass.

"The voices got worse. They were coming from inside the walls, whispering things to me, horrible things. They said they were going to hurt May, and they'd describe the awful things they were going to do to her. I started picking away at the walls—just a little bit at first, but then making the hole bigger and bigger. I hid it with a poster, because deep down I guess I knew things weren't right in my head, but I didn't know how to stop it.

"But the voices kept coming. They were telling me how they could move through the walls of the building to get into May's room down the hall. They said they were watching her sleep, and talked about how helpless she was, and how they could do all these awful things to her—" Her voice broke, and she clamped a hand over her mouth, trying to contain her emotions enough to continue. Ellen was still watching her in horror, like she was a car crash she couldn't quite bring herself to look away from. They'd known each other for two years, and Liv had never made a single mention of the mental health problems that had plagued her for most of her life.

"I tried to find them—the people the voices belonged to—but every time I thought I'd managed to catch one of them in the walls, they always slipped away. I started to think of how I could get them out, how I could force them to come out, and I came up with a plan. I knew when they were in there, because they told me how they liked to watch May sleep, so I decided the night time was the best option. I stuffed a whole heap of crunched up paper in the hole I'd created in my bedroom wall, and then I set fire to it with a lighter. I hadn't thought the flames would catch on so quickly. My plan was to smoke them out, that was all. To make it so they weren't able to breathe in there, and they'd be forced to come out. I hadn't known how quickly the flames would spread, but they caught up inside the walls of the student halls and tore straight through them. The building was old, and there was something they'd used when they'd created all the dividing walls for the student bedrooms that should never have passed fire regulations. But because it was inside the walls, I didn't even realise how badly it had spread until everything started to bubble and peel."

She shook her head and covered her face with her hands.

"Jesus Christ," Ellen muttered, horrified. She picked up the empty bottle of water in her shaking hand and tried to drain the last dregs, only to find it empty.

"When I realised what was happening, that I hadn't smoked anyone out, but instead had set fire to the student halls,

I ran. I banged on all the doors, but it all happened so fast. We were three stories up, so everyone started to converge on the stairwell, pushing and shoving each other to get down the stairs. Some people had already got in the lift, but then it got stuck, and we could hear the students screaming inside. It was chaos. I couldn't tell if May was with everyone, and the heat and flames had got so bad by then I couldn't go back to check."

"I remember that happening," Ellen said, aghast. "It was in the student accommodation in Manchester."

Liv nodded. "I was lucky. No one died, but May was severely burned. She lost all the hair from one side of her head and had to go through numerous skin grafts. It could have been worse, but there isn't a day that goes by when I'm not eaten up with guilt about what I did. I ended up in a psychiatric unit for five years. When I got out, I moved to London and became Olivia."

"Your guilt didn't stop you hurting me, though," Ellen said, tears in her eyes. "You forgot all about what you did when you were drugging me and locking me inside here."

"I'm sorry, Ellen. I'm so sorry. I thought I was keeping you safe."

"Just like that poor girl you burned at university," she spat. "You're sick, Liv. You need help."

"I know, I know." She put her face in her hands again and sobbed, great, heart-wrenching sobs. Ellen made no move to comfort her, and she didn't blame her in the slightest. She didn't deserve any comfort, not after everything she'd done.

"I saw Zach," she managed to say eventually. "I was with Michael in the city, and he saw me and recognised me. I was so frightened he was going to tell Michael what I'd done, and then everyone would know what a terrible person I was. I thought he was following me, that he planned some kind of revenge for what I'd done to May."

"It's a shame he wasn't, because then maybe none of this would have ever happened."

Ellen got to her feet, putting her hands out either side to support herself against the wardrobe walls as she staggered out on weak, trembling legs. "I'm going to call the police now, Liv, and I don't want you to stop me."

"I won't," she said, her voice barely a whisper.

And she stayed that way, kneeling on the wardrobe floor, until the police arrived to take her away.

Chapter Thirty-six
Six Weeks Later

OLIVIA LAY ON THE NARROW bed of her hospital room, staring up at the ceiling.

She was feeling better now, though the drugs they gave her dulled her senses and made it so she didn't quite feel like herself. The doctors told her it wouldn't be forever, just long enough to make sure the drugs were working, and then they'd be able to start to reduce the dosage again.

It wasn't so bad here. She was allowed to feed the fish kept in a tank in the common room and help serve up the meals, as long as she made sure each patient got the same amount and didn't play favourites. Liv didn't have any favourites. She kept herself distant from everyone else, knowing her and friendships didn't mix so well. It was fine. She was happy with her own company.

A knock came at her door, and she half sat.

"You have a visitor, Olivia," said one of the nurses.

She sat up straighter. Her parents had been here a few days earlier, and she wasn't expecting anyone else.

Olivia climbed off the bed and left her room to go to the common room where the patients met with visitors.

Her heart jolted as she spotted a familiar blonde head. As though she'd sensed her enter, Ellen turned in her seat.

The two women locked eyes, and Liv's breath caught. She'd come here to see her, but what would she say? Would it be anger and accusations? She couldn't blame Ellen if she hated her and was furious with her. After what she'd done, she deserved it, but that didn't make it any easier to take.

Olivia took a seat opposite her ex-best friend. "You've come to see me?"

Ellen nodded. "Yes, I have. This doesn't mean we're friends, though."

"Then why are you here?"

Ellen gave a shrug. "I'm not sure. Closure, I guess. I wanted to see how you were. I understand that you were sick and you didn't do what you did to hurt me."

Tears filled Liv's eyes. She'd cried so much over the past six weeks. Even the numbness from the drugs hadn't been able to stop the tears. "I'm so sorry, Elles. I should have got help sooner. If I'd realised, I would have. I swear to you. There were signs, and I shouldn't have ignored them, but I didn't do it intentionally."

She nodded. "I know that."

"How's Michael?" she dared to ask. "Have you seen or spoken to him at all?"

"Only the once since you were committed. His wife found out everything, of course. It wasn't only you he was cheating on her with. He'd been sleeping with his secretary, too. It came out because one of his work colleagues had caught him having sex with her over his desk. Apparently Michael had begged him not to say anything, and claimed it was a one-off, but then when everything came out about you, it was all over the papers, and his colleague spilled the beans, too."

Liv gave a cold laugh. "He told me about that during one of our early dates, but he said he was the one who had caught the colleague and the secretary."

"Wow." Ellen pulled a face. "That guy certainly had some nerve, right? I mean, I know he didn't deserve what you did to him any more than I did, but it really couldn't have happened to a nicer guy."

Liv didn't miss the sarcasm in her tone.

"Even if he was a terrible person, it still doesn't excuse what I did." Her hands rested on the table between them, and she picked at the dried skin around her nails, picking, picking, picking, until specks of blood appeared against her skin.

"No, it doesn't, but you didn't do anything out of hate, Liv. You did it because you thought it was for the best."

She lifted her gaze to meet Ellen's. "Didn't I? What about Tammy? What about Holly Newie? How do we know I didn't hurt them? I still don't remember what happened during those blackouts. Maybe I never will."

"You just latched onto Holly Newie because you were sick, Liv. Michael still insists he's never even met the woman, and I tend to believe him. And as for Tammy, well, you know what she was like. I spoke to Tammy's mother when we cleared out the flat. She's heartbroken but not surprised it came to this. Tammy had a history of drug abuse that goes back to her teenage years."

"She did?"

Ellen nodded. "Yes, she did. It had nothing to do with you. It was just bad luck that the two of you ended up living together."

It occurred to Liv that she and Tammy had had more in common than they'd realised. Perhaps if either of them had actually opened up about who they really were, they might have even been friends.

"What about you?" Liv asked. "How have you been, after everything?"

She nodded and glanced down. "I'm okay. Suffering from nightmares and panic attacks, but they're getting better."

"I'm so sorry," she whispered, looking down at her hands again.

"I saw Ryan and the new woman," Ellen continued. "She has a bump now, and she was ordering Ryan around like she was an invalid, and he was chasing around after her, doing everything she said."

Liv bit her lower lip. "I'm sorry about that, too. About not telling you sooner."

Ellen shrugged. "It's fine. I understand why you didn't. You kind of had a lot going on in that head of yours. It was Ryan's fault for cheating on me in the first place, not yours. You should never have been burdened with his lies on top of everything else."

"So, you forgive me for that part, at least?" she asked hopefully.

"Yes, for that part." Ellen gave a sigh. "Look, I don't want you to get the wrong idea. I'm not going to make a habit of visiting you."

"I know that," she said, her voice small.

"You understand why we can't be friends anymore, don't you, Liv?" She shook her head. "I mean Sarah." Ellen gave a small, nervous laugh. "I don't know what to call you anymore."

"Liv," Olivia said. "I changed my name legally. It's still Liv."

She nodded. "Okay, good. It feels weird to call you something else. Anyway, I just wanted to come and say goodbye."

"Thank you for coming."

Ellen got to her feet and gave Liv one final, tight smile before turning away and walking from the common room.

Olivia stayed where she was for a moment, trying to keep her emotions in check. She didn't trust her emotions. If she lost the small grip she had on herself, she didn't think she would ever get it back again.

Movement in front of her caught her attention, and, for the briefest of moments, she thought Ellen had come back again. But then she saw it was one of the other patients, a blonde woman a couple of years younger than she was, who she'd seen around but hadn't spoken to.

"Was that your friend?" the young woman asked.

Liv nodded, not trusting herself to speak just yet.

The blonde woman smiled. "You know, it would be nice to have a friend in here, too. I've seen you around, and I thought you looked like my kind of person."

Olivia allowed a small smile to touch her lips. "You have?" It was all she ever wanted, just to be liked, to be accepted.

"Of course." The blonde stuck her hand across the table. "My name's Grace."

Liv hesitated for a moment and then shook it. "Hello, Grace. I'm Olivia."

Acknowledgments

Writing a book can be somewhat of a solitary process, but the actual creation of a book, and bringing it to publication, involves a whole team of people. There are a lot of folks I need to thank, so bear with me, and if I've missed anyone, it's because I have a terrible memory, not that I didn't appreciate you!

Thank you to my long time editor, Lori Whitwam, and my proofreaders, Tammy Payne, Linda Helme, and Karey Mc-Comish, for your sharp eyes. Many thanks to my first reader on this book, Glynis Elliott, for all your encouragement. Hearing those words 'it's the best thing you've written' is ultimately what I strive for. I was thrilled you loved *Some They Lie* so much.

Thank you to fellow authors Mel Comley and Shalini Boland, for allowing me to pick your brains when necessary, and for all of your support as well. I'm truly grateful.

Many thanks to my friend Kelly Forrester for your advice when it came to how an estate agents works, and for your suggestions, even though it wasn't *that* kind of book! And thank you to everyone who helped me with the mental health aspect and hospital procedures. You shall remain anonymous, but not forgotten!

And a final massive thank you to Rachel McClellan, who showed me just how generous the author community can be. I may not have finished this book if it hadn't been for you.

And thank you to you, the reader, for reading and supporting me. I hope you enjoyed the book.

Marissa.

About the Author

M.K. Farrar is the pen name for a USA Today Bestselling author of more than thirty novels. 'Some They Lie' is her first psychological thriller, but won't be her last. When she's not writing, M.K. is rescuing animals from far off places, binge watching shows on Netflix, or reading. She lives in the English countryside with her husband, three daughters, and menagerie of pets.

You can sign up to MK's newsletter here - https://landing.mailerlite.com/webforms/landing/m6v9h8

Or she can be emailed at mkfarrar@hotmail.com. She loves to hear from readers!

Printed in Great Britain
by Amazon